BOW STREET BARON

The Castleburys
Book 5

By Jennifer Seasons

Dragonblade Publishing, Inc. is an imprint of Kathryn Le Veque Novels, Inc.
P.O. Box 23
Moreno Valley, CA 92556
ceo@dragonbladepublishing.com

Produced in the United States of America

First Edition September 2024
Trade Paperback Edition

ARE YOU SIGNED UP FOR DRAGONBLADE'S BLOG?

You'll get the latest news and information on exclusive giveaways, exclusive excerpts, coming releases, sales, free books, cover reveals and more.

Check out our complete list of authors, too!

No spam, no junk. That's a promise!

Sign Up Here

www.dragonbladepublishing.com

Dearest Reader;

Thank you for your support of a small press. At Dragonblade Publishing, we strive to bring you the highest quality Historical Romance from some of the best authors in the business. Without your support, there is no 'us', so we sincerely hope you adore these stories and find some new favorite authors along the way.

Happy Reading!

CEO, Dragonblade Publishing

Additional Dragonblade books by Author Jennifer Seasons

The Castleburys Series
Mayfair Misfit (Book 1)
Duke Undone (Book 2)
Dockside Duchess (Book 3)
London's Leading Lady (Book 4)
Bow Street Baron (Book 5)

CHAPTER ONE

November 1832
Madame Toussaint's Modiste Shop
Bond Street, London

"I TELL YOU true and honest, the Revivalists are primed to attack again."

Juliette sighed. Them again.

Couldn't the ladies discuss something else—*anything* else?

"Marianne, you ninny, how could you possibly know such things? Have you direct knowledge of their evil plans?" A haughty scoff came from the overstuffed bench along the near wall. "I think not. Not with the way you bury your nose in every novel that flits your way. You've a mind filled with fiction, you have. The Revivalists are no more likely to attack this night because you say so than I am to leap across the crest of the moon."

"*That* I would look up from my novel to witness if you could indeed achieve such a feat, sister dear."

"You are decidedly aggravating."

"Yet not wrong about the Revivalists," Marianne Martingale pointed out with a prim, satisfied smile. "They are set to pounce again at any moment, scattering all of us like mice away from a hungry stray cat."

Inwardly recoiling, Juliette flinched while she pinned and tucked her finest rose silk across the bust of Marianne, pretending to ignore the young ladies' unguarded chatter. The Revivalists.

Mon Dieu, she hoped it was not true! Those murdering aristocrats had spent the better part of a year terrorizing London before a long, blessedly silent hiatus. After their massive attack on Seven Dials nearly three years ago, the group had gone quiet for a time, leading authorities and citizens alike to hope they had disbanded and quit—or, best of all, were *dead*.

The way they had made so many other people.

Mark her—even if it made her an awful person for thinking so, she had hoped it was the latter. It was no more than they deserved.

A chill suddenly swept down Juliette's spine, and she sucked in a breath, hand jerking in reflex.

"Ouch!" cried Marianne.

"*Excusez-moi*, I'm so sorry!" Juliette said in her lightly accented voice, her hazel eyes flicking up to catch the flash of pain rippling across Marianne's freckled countenance. "That was clumsy of me." As proprietress of the shop, she knew better than to stab a customer with a pin! It never boded well for repeat business.

Perhaps that was what she deserved for having such unkind thoughts.

Juliette continued her work, focusing on not stabbing her client. The rose silk, soft and luxurious, draped elegantly over Marianne's form, her discomfort momentarily forgotten amidst the whispers of danger and intrigue as the young debutante listened eagerly to the gossip around her.

"Primed to attack again, you say? The Revivalists?" queried Lady Eugenia Hartfield, a statuesque woman wearing a gown of azure satin, its voluminous skirts swishing with every indignant turn she made. "This city has become a hotbed of sensationalist tales. Every gossip rag abounds with them. Do tell me, when did you become an oracle, Marianne?"

"Oh, hush, Eugenia. There's no need for sarcasm. I heard it from Lady Henrietta's footman, and you know they hear everything," Marianne retorted, a challenging glint in her eyes.

"And you believe a footman's gossip is reliable information?" Lady Eugenia scoffed, dabbing a delicate lace handkerchief at her powdered nose.

"Of course I do!" Marianne returned. "Staff know everyone's business. Who doesn't accept that fact? That's why Mother shoos the help from the room when Mr. Hanvelian comes to visit."

Juliette, needle in hand, listened with keen interest. The Revivalists, a name she had tried to erase from her memory, surged back with a vengeance. Her heart quickened, though she couldn't pinpoint why. Confusion shrouded her past like the morning fog, leaving her with fragments of a life. Not even enough to hold on to. Just enough to know it was there. Nagging. Haunting. Day in and out for the past three years. It was exhausting.

As she continued the delicate dance of pinning fabric, she overheard snippets of conversation—of whispered threats, masked identities, and the urgency of Captain Catamount Castlebury's pursuit. The mere mention of the Bow Street Runner sent shivers of a different kind down her spine, a reaction unexplained by her forgetful mind.

"Captain Castlebury has sworn to put an end to their reign of terror. I hear he's closing in," Lady Eugenia remarked, her tone full of admiration. "I certainly hope so, for all our sakes."

Juliette's fingers trembled slightly. She redirected her attention to her work, attempting to stifle the unease clawing at the edges of her consciousness.

"That Captain Castlebury is a dashing hero, no doubt," gushed Isabella Martingale from nearby the velvet selections, a vision in lavender silk, her blonde ringlets bouncing as she spoke. "I heard he single-handedly faced down a group of ruffians in Whitechapel. Such bravery!"

"Bravery or foolhardiness, I wonder," Lady Eugenia mused, a skeptical arch to her perfectly groomed eyebrow. "Regardless, it's heartening to know someone is taking action. We can't have our city overrun by such scoundrels. It's bad for the complexion."

As the lively chatter of the customers echoed through the

shop, Juliette worked tirelessly, her mind wrestling with the conflicting emotions stirred by the mention of the Revivalists and the enigmatic Captain Castlebury. Her hands moved with practiced grace, concealing the turmoil within her.

"I heard from Lady Felicity that the poor souls in Spitalfields were utterly defenseless when the Revivalists attacked," exclaimed Lady Penelope, Countess de Winter, dressed in a gown of delicate lace and intricate embroidery. Juliette recognized it from last year's set. A year later it still held up. Because she did great work. "Those brutes descended upon them like a pack of wolves."

Juliette continued to work on Miss Marianne's gown. The rose silk seemed to mock her, a reminder of a world that trembled under the threat of violence. The mention of Spitalfields sent a chill through her, and she struggled to focus on the delicate task before her. *Breathe, Juliette.*

"Imagine the audacity of attacking in broad daylight!" gasped Isabella, younger sister to Marianne, her gloved hands fluttering to her chest. "One can't even stroll through Spitalfields without fearing for one's life. Not that I'm strolling through Spitalfields, mind you. But still, it's positively scandalous."

A vivid image flashed in Juliette's mind, an image she couldn't fully grasp, and she gasped. Shadows, faces, and the echo of distant screams danced on the periphery of her memory, teasing her with fragments of a past she couldn't quite piece together. Spitalfields? Attacks? What was happening with her mind?

Lady Eugenia, overhearing Juliette's subtle gasp, said, "Madame Toussaint, you seem quite affected by the tales of the Revivalists. Is there something amiss?"

Juliette struggled to maintain her composure, the swell of anxiety threatening to engulf her. "N-nothing, Lady Eugenia. Merely the musings of a city haunted by shadows," she stammered, feigning a nonchalance that barely concealed her unease. She brushed a lone auburn lock of hair from her cheek and offered a small smile.

"Did you hear they left a calling card at the scene in Spital-fields? A morbid token of their handiwork," revealed Lady Penelope, her eyes wide with a mix of horror and interest. "It's a new development in their behavior."

"Captain Castlebury will make them pay for their atrocities, mark my words," declared Isabella, her eyes ablaze with unwavering confidence in the Bow Street Runner. Clearly the youngest Martingale possessed *admiration* for the detective.

Captain Castlebury—his name echoed in Juliette's mind like a distant drumbeat. She fought to comprehend why his pursuit of the Revivalists stirred a profound, disconcerting reaction within her. Her heart raced, and beads of sweat formed on her forehead. Just his name made her ache deep down inside. Why?

Attempting to divert her thoughts, she focused back on her work, desperate to finish pinning the rose silk gown. Yet the threads of fear, woven into the fabric of the conversation, entangled her, making each stitch a laborious effort. Her fingers felt clumsy. Thick.

She felt the weight of the conversation pressing on her, an invisible burden that demanded a reprieve. With a forced smile, she excused herself, mentioning the need for a specific thread to complete Marianne's gown. As she retreated into the backroom, the door closed with a muted thud, leaving her alone in the sanctuary of dimly lit solitude. Leaning against the door, she let out a shaky breath. Her palms still sweaty, she pressed a fist against her stomach, attempting to quell the riotous storm within. The voices of the customers, their tales of the Revivalists, still echoed in her ears, and she couldn't escape the lingering unease that clung to her like a bad stench.

"*Mon Dieu*, what is happening to me?" she muttered, searching the room as if the answers she sought were hidden within its walls. She tried to piece together the fragments of her life beyond the last three years. It was like trying to grasp at smoke—elusive, fleeting, and frustratingly insubstantial.

She paced the small room, her footsteps echoing against the

wooden floor. The air seemed charged with a strange energy, of fear and uncertainty. Juliette continued to mutter to herself, her words a desperate attempt to anchor herself in the turbulent sea of her memories. "I remember Bond Street, the shop, the delicate fabrics from France. I remember the past three years and nothing more. But who am I? What happened three years ago, and why can't I remember my life before then?" She ran a hand through her auburn hair, questions tumbling swiftly through her mind. "Why do I fear the Revivalists, and why does Captain Castlebury's name resonate in my heart?"

As Juliette spoke, a soft rustling interrupted her soliloquy. From behind a stack of small boxes containing laces and threads, a tiny, fluffy kitten emerged, blinking sleepily. Its fur, a blend of whites, grays, and delicate patches of orange, created a stark contrast to the seriousness that filled the room. Such sweetness amongst all this grim talk. "Well, *la petit* Odette," she sighed, a slight smile breaking through the tension on her face. She knelt down and sat on the floor, gently stroking the kitten's fur. "At least you don't carry the weight of forgotten memories. Do you?"

The kitten, seemingly content in Juliette's presence, purred softly. It curled around her fingers, a warm, comforting presence in the midst of her confusion.

"Perhaps you hold the key to unlocking the mysteries of my past," she mused, half joking. Yet there was a hint of genuine curiosity in her voice as she continued to speak to her fluffy companion. "If only you could talk, my dear, you might unravel the threads of my forgotten life."

Odette, oblivious to Juliette's internal struggle, nuzzled against her hand, providing a small but tangible comfort.

Cradling the kitten against her chest, she surveyed the room she called her own. The low light revealed the intricate details of her attire, reflecting her keen sense of fashion.

She wore a gown of rich emerald-green silk that cascaded gracefully around her curves. The bodice was adorned with delicate lace, expertly embroidered by her own hands, drawing attention to her slender waist. The sleeves, puffed at the shoulders, tapered elegantly down to her wrists, each cuff decorated with tiny pearl buttons. The skirt flowed in soft, graceful folds, pooling around her as she sat beside a vintage chaise longue, an exquisite piece from a bygone era. Her hair, a cascade of rich auburn waves, fell in loose curls around her shoulders. A few strands were artfully pulled back with a delicate ribbon, allowing her freckled face to be illuminated by the soft glow of the room. The freckles, like tiny constellations, speckled her nose and cheeks, adding a touch of whimsy to her otherwise composed appearance.

Juliette took a deep breath, the sensation of the kitten's warmth against her chest grounding her in the present moment. She looked around at the eclectic assortment of fabrics, ribbons, and trinkets that filled the backroom of her modiste shop. It was a space she had meticulously curated, a place of creativity and elegance. "You know, my little friend," she murmured to Odette, a gentle smile playing on her lips, "I may not remember everything, but I have built a life here—a life surrounded by beauty and grace. That much is evident."

Odette blinked up at her, as if understanding the comforting words spoken in her direction.

Juliette continued, a sense of gratitude rising within her, offsetting the swirling anxiety. "I have this shop, these fabrics from France, and the joy of making one-of-a-kind, exquisite gowns for the women of London. Yes, there's an unease, a fear that lingers in the shadows that I don't understand, but perhaps that's the price one pays for the blessings we have." She gently stroked Odette's fur, feeling the rise and fall of the kitten's contented breathing. "You remind me to appreciate the simple joys—like the softness of your fur and the companionship you offer. Perhaps, in these small moments, I can find the peace I seek."

Perhaps that was all anyone truly had—small moments.

Small moments strung together, one after the other, to make

a full life.

She gazed around her creative haven and resolved to embrace the beauty that surrounded her, finding centeredness in the present even as the ghosts of her past lingered in the dark corners. Juliette squared her shoulders, shaking off the lingering unease that had clung to her moments ago. Standing, she gave Odette one last snuggle and set her to rest on the chaise. "Nap well, *petit chat.*"

As she opened the door to return to the main part of the shop, the atmosphere shifted. The lively chatter of the customers continued, but a palpable excitement filled the air. Something, or rather *someone*, had captured their attention.

"It's him!"

"Shh, don't let him hear you!"

"I doubt verily that he can hear me through the glass."

"With your shrill voice, I would be shocked if he cannot."

"Move so I may have a better view of him. Ouch! Drat it all, Isabella, that was my foot."

"Well, I'm not giving away my prime viewing location. Find your own to ogle him."

"Oh, that Captain Castlebury. He's so manly," came the voice of Lady Penelope.

Juliette came down the hall and stopped dead in her tracks, eyes widening with disbelief. "It *is* him."

There, outside the expansive front window of her shop, stood Captain Catamount Castlebury. The subject of gossip just moments ago now materialized before her very eyes, a mysterious, impossibly handsome presence in the London fog clinging to Bond Street outside.

Though she had not met him before, her everything lit up inside at the sight of him.

Recognition. Her everything recognized him.

But how?

His appearance matched the vivid descriptions she had heard—the tawny, sun-kissed, shaggy hair, pale green eyes that seemed to pierce through the foggy gloom, and the long outer jacket that accentuated his rugged, tough physique. His tall, broad-shouldered frame commanded attention, and the ladies within the shop erupted into another chorus of delighted whispers at the sight of him.

"You move."

"No, *you* move!"

"Why, he is utterly delicious to gaze upon, isn't he?" This from Lady Eugenia in a shockingly adoring tone.

"Aren't you married?" Countess de Winters inquired with surprise.

"Widowed like you, two seasons past. I'm fully allowed to enjoy this unexpected delight, Penelope."

"Of course. As you were, dearest. Of particular note, his thighs are rather robust and hearty. Good for certain activities, you understand."

"Indeed, I do. *Indeed.*" The way Lady Eugenia drew out the word made it sound rather indecent.

If Juliette hadn't catered to aristocratic ladies every day for at least the past three years, she might have been shocked by the discussion. As it stood, she barely noted the crudeness anymore.

Suddenly the room seemed to blur around her as her heart skipped a beat, caught in a rhythm the Bow Street captain seemed to dictate as she stared at him through the front window. She had never met him, didn't know him personally, and yet an inexplicable connection tugged at her from within—and it led straight toward him. A magnetic pull that defied reason and logic. A gasp escaped her lips, barely audible amidst the excited tittering of the ladies.

Captain Castlebury stood out there on the sidewalk in front of her shop engaged in conversation with a nearby shopkeeper, his confident demeanor and authoritative presence casting a spell over all the ladies inside. Maybe it was the gold-tipped hair. Maybe it was the rugged confidence. Or the acre-wide shoulders. Or the—well, yes—*thighs*. Whatever it was, *ton* ladies could not get enough.

And neither, apparently, could she.

As her customers gossiped around her, Juliette found herself rooted to the spot, her gaze fixed on the man whose very name stirred emotions she couldn't comprehend. The urge to run to him, to seek refuge in the embrace of a stranger, overwhelmed her. That she instinctively knew she would be welcome was even more odd. Unsettling. *Upsetting.*

"He's even more handsome in person!" exclaimed Isabella, her blue eyes sparkling with admiration.

"He looks like he could handle those Revivalists single-handedly," remarked Lady Eugenia. "All those *muscles.*"

Juliette snorted at that and struggled to regain her composure. The presence of Captain Castlebury, so close yet still a stranger, sent a ripple of conflicting emotions through her. Trying to quell the fluttering in her chest, she forced herself to move forward, joining the group of ladies who gathered near the window, their eyes fixated on the charismatic Bow Street Runner.

"He's positively dashing, isn't he?" Lady Penelope said, fanning herself delicately with her lace handkerchief.

"He looks like a man who's seen his fair share of danger," added Marianne, narrowing her eyes with obvious curiosity.

"He's the only one who will put an end to the Revivalists' reign of terror," one of the other ladies whispered, a sentiment echoed by the others.

Juliette, still captivated by the scene outside, nodded along absently. A part of her mind urged her to break away from this fascination, to focus on the tasks at hand in her shop. Yet an irresistible force kept her bound in the moment, her eyes drawn to the man who represented both danger and an elusive connection to her past. Somehow she just knew it.

A gust of wind ruffled Captain Castlebury's hair as he turned, catching her gaze through the window. Their eyes locked for a brief, electrifying moment, and something unspoken passed between them. As if the currents of destiny whispered secrets that her conscious mind couldn't decipher.

The ladies continued to gossip around her, but Juliette felt a strange detachment. She finally tore her gaze away from the Bow Street captain, focusing on the vibrant colors of the fabrics in her shop. Taking a deep breath, she willed herself to push aside the inexplicable emotions and concentrate on the practical matters at hand. It was hard, but thankfully, she managed.

"Come, ladies, let us return to the fitting room," Juliette suggested, her voice betraying no hint of the chaos within. "There are gowns to be fitted and beauties to adorn."

And handsome Bow Street Runners to avoid daydreaming about.

CHAPTER TWO

CATAMOUNT SAT IN his office at the Bow Street Runners' headquarters, the atmosphere outside his door charged with urgency and the low hum of activity. A stack of papers sat before him, the file on the Revivalists open and haunting. Three years had passed since the tragic attack on Seven Dials, and the wounds inflicted on his heart were still raw.

His fingers drummed a restless rhythm on the polished surface of the desk. The loss of his Julie that night had left him hollow, aching for justice and closure. The memories of that dreadful attack played like a haunting melody in the recesses of his mind. "Julie," he whispered, the syllables heavy with grief. His eyes lingered on a faded likeness of her, tucked within the pages of the file—one of his that he had placed there. Julie's laughter, her warmth—those were the things he carried within him, a bittersweet burden that fueled his determination to capture the Revivalists. "They won't escape justice. I swear it," he muttered to himself, the words a solemn vow. He clenched his jaw with resolve as he traced the details of the Seven Dials attack in the file. Faces of the victims, the devastation wrought by the Revivalists— it all etched a painful tableau in his memory.

The Revivalists, those aristocratic madmen who had terror- ized London, were still at large, their malevolent presence casting a shadow over the city. "Three years, and they've eluded capture. But not for much longer," he declared, the timbre of his voice resonating with unwavering commitment. He clenched his hand into a fist, nails digging into his palm as he steeled himself against the ache of his loss. You would think he'd be used to it by now.

The activity outside his office door intensified, the clamor of voices and hurried footsteps a constant reminder of the importance of his mission. Catamount's gaze shifted from the file to the city beyond his window—a city he had sworn to protect. As he continued to sift through the evidence, memories of Julie—her vibrant spirit, and the promises they had made—taunted him. The room pulsed with his unspoken anguish.

As he sat back in his chair, the weight of the past pressed heavily on his shoulders. The room, filled with the muted sounds of activity outside, seemed to close in around him. Anger, weariness, and cynicism mingled in his gut as he stared at the file before him. "Julie," he murmured once more, the name a whispered lament that hung in the air. The ache of her absence felt like a perpetual wound, a hole in his being that would never heal. He missed her with a depth that words could hardly capture.

A soft knock interrupted the heavy silence, and Lieutenant Harcourt entered cautiously. His expression showed respect and concern as he approached Catamount's desk. "Captain, I hope I'm not disturbing you," Harcourt began.

Catamount sighed, running a hand through his hair. "Speak your mind, lieutenant. I've grown accustomed to disturbances."

Harcourt hesitated for a moment before continuing. "The men are restless, sir. They're looking to you for direction. The Revivalists' latest attack in Spitalfields has stirred unease, and the city is on edge."

A cynical smile played on Catamount's lips. "Unease? London has been on edge for years. The Revivalists' reign of terror sees to that."

His lieutenant nodded, acknowledging the bitter truth. "We've received reports of increased activity, whispers in the shadows. The people want justice, sir."

Justice. Julie's name echoed in his mind again, a reminder of the justice denied to her. Catamount leaned back, studying Harcourt with a tired gaze. "Justice is a scarce commodity, lieutenant. The Revivalists are elusive, cunning. But we'll press on."

Harcourt shifted uncomfortably, sensing the weight of his captain's burden. "The men need a leader, sir. Someone to inspire confidence and quell the rising fear."

Catamount's eyes narrowed, his cynicism deepening. "Fear is a potent weapon, lieutenant. It lingers in the shadows, waiting to be exploited. But I'll address the men. Tell them to prepare for what lies ahead."

Harcourt saluted. "Very good." He turned to leave but stopped. "I keep hearing the men call you baron," he said, turning back around. "What am I missing?"

Catamount smirked and waved a dismissive hand. "Merely the tedious and long explanation of a highly complicated entailed title bestowed upon me."

His lieutenant nodded. "Thank you for sparing me."

"You're welcome."

Harcourt lingered near the door, his eyes fixed on Catamount's troubled expression. "What is it?"

"Something's bothering me about the Seven Dials attack, lieutenant," Catamount admitted, his voice low and measured. "There's a detail, a thread I can't quite unravel. It's been gnawing at me, keeping me awake at night."

Harcourt furrowed his brow. "Sir, you've dedicated everything to solving that case. What could be amiss?"

Catamount shook his head. "I can't put my finger on it. It's like a shadow just beyond reach. I've scrutinized every report, every statement, but there's a missing piece."

"Perhaps a fresh perspective, sir? Someone to review the case with a new set of eyes."

Catamount considered the suggestion, his mind grappling with the prospect of seeking external aid. "I've been through every detail countless times. It's not about fresh eyes, but about catching a glimpse of something I might have overlooked." He leaned back in his chair. "The loss of Julie clouds my judgment. I can't shake the feeling that there's more to the Seven Dials attack, something we've missed."

Harcourt stepped forward. "Captain, you can't shoulder this burden alone. The entire force is at your disposal. We'll find the truth of that night, sir."

A bitter smile touched Catamount's lips. "Truth, lieutenant, is a slippery thing. But we'll do what we can. Notify the men— prepare them for heightened surveillance. We can't afford any missteps."

Harcourt saluted once more before leaving the room, leaving Catamount alone with the weight of his thoughts. The room felt suffocating, the air heavy with the unresolved mysteries that lingered in the aftermath of the Seven Dials attack. The elusive truth seemed to dance just out of reach, taunting him in the silence of his sleepless nights.

Catamount tossed the file on his desk with frustration, and the parchment rustled in protest against the polished surface. Scrubbing a large, callused hand over his face, he felt the weariness settle deep within his bones. The burdens of the past and the relentless pursuit of justice had taken their toll. "Christ, I'm tired," he muttered to himself, the words a gritty admission of his soul-deep exhaustion. He longed for nights when sleep wasn't elusive, and dreams didn't weave a tapestry of memories he wished he could forget.

His gaze drifted back to the file, the details of the attack staring back at him like accusing specters. Leaning back in his chair, he muttered aloud, as if the walls held the key to the truth that eluded him, "What is it that's not sitting right?" The question hung in the air, unanswered. He retraced the events of that fateful night, trying to pinpoint the detail that eluded him, the thread that remained just out of reach.

Julie's face, her laughter, haunted him like a phantom. "What did I miss, my love?" he whispered, as if she could hear him from beyond the veil. He longed for the comfort of her presence, the warmth that had been stolen from him by the Revivalists.

With a heavy sigh, Catamount raked a hand through his shaggy hair again. The file lay open before him, unanswered questions gnawing at him. The road ahead seemed endless, the pursuit of justice an unrelenting journey through the labyrinth of the past.

"Is the captain in his office? I'm taking him to lunch."

Catamount looked up at the sound of the familiar voice, a welcome distraction from his brooding thoughts. Standing in the doorway was his brother, Crawford, the new Earl of Castlebury, with his pale blue eyes and glossy auburn hair. Dapper as ever, Crawford exuded an air of sophistication that contrasted with Catamount's worn demeanor.

"Ah, the prodigal brother appears," Catamount said, managing a faint smile. "Late lunch, you say? I'm afraid the only thing on my plate is the lingering mystery of the Seven Dials attack."

Crawford strolled into the room, scanning the papers scattered across Catamount's desk. "Still haunted by that, are you? You need a break, Cat. London won't fall apart if you step away for a moment, I promise."

Catamount leaned back in his chair, studying his brother's concerned expression. "The city might not crumble, but justice eludes us. There's something about that night... something I can't grasp. It's grinding at me and keeping me up at night."

Crawford pulled up a chair, his posture elegant even in casual conversation. "You've been working tirelessly, Cat. Perhaps a respite is in order. Clear your mind. You look like you could use some fresh air."

Catamount sighed. "Maybe you're right. A late lunch wouldn't go amiss. I probably do need to step away from this for a moment."

Crawford came to him and clapped him on the shoulder. "That's the spirit, old chap. A change of scenery might do wonders for your perspective."

"But I can't. I have to keep working."

"Cat, you can't keep pushing yourself like this," his brother insisted. "You're starting to look like a ghost, and I doubt you've had a decent meal in days."

Catamount shrugged off Crawford's hand from his shoulder, his gaze fixed on the bustling activity of Bow Street through the window beyond them. "I'll eat later. The city needs safekeeping."

Crawford's expression softened. "Justice won't be served if you're running on fumes. You're no good to anyone if you collapse from exhaustion."

"I can handle it," Catamount retorted, his voice clipped. "I won't let Julie's memory be tarnished by letting these murderers go free."

His brother sighed. "Cat, Julie wouldn't want to see you destroy yourself over this. Taking a break doesn't mean you're giving up. It means you're giving yourself a chance to regroup."

"I don't need a break. I need answers. I need to make sure no one else suffers the way Julie did."

Crawford shook his head. "I just worry about you, that's all. You're not invincible."

Catamount's scowl remained. "I appreciate your concern, but I've got work to do. You can go to lunch without me."

"Fine. But you'll join us at the Meadowlark Tavern later for drinks. Rainville and Damon will be there. It's not negotiable."

Catamount continued to scowl but nodded begrudgingly. "I'll make an appearance. But don't expect me to stay long. There's work to be done."

His brother gave a satisfied smile, knowing that getting Catamount to agree to even a brief respite was a small victory. "Excellent. The change might do you some good. We'll be waiting for you."

With that, Crawford left Catamount to his duties. As the door closed, Catamount sighed, his mind already drifting back to the unsolved mysteries and the shadows of the past that refused to release their grip.

The promise of drinks at the Meadowlark Tavern loomed in the distance, a rare opportunity for camaraderie. Reluctantly, he acknowledged that a brief diversion might be what he needed, even if only to appease his concerned brother.

CHAPTER THREE

JULIETTE'S EYES SNAPPED open, and she found herself in the dimly lit bedchamber of her small flat above the modiste shop. Odette nestled on her chest, providing a comforting presence. However, the tendrils of a haunting nightmare still lingered, casting gloom over her senses.

A cascade of her hair tumbled loosely around her as she tried to make sense of the room, her heart pounding furiously in her chest, panic still gripping her. The lace curtains swayed gently, revealing the evening outside, but the warm glow failed to dispel the chill that clung to her skin. Dressed in a simple nightgown, Juliette traced the cotton fabric with anxious fingers, seeking a grounding touch. The room, with its Parisian paintings and delicate trinkets, offered little solace as she grappled with the aftermath of the nightmare. *Breathe, just breathe. Slowly, in and out.*

Odette purred, a soothing sound that contrasted with the turmoil within Juliette. Suddenly a memory, dark and fearful, and an unsettling metallic scent overcame her, and she gave a startled sob, terror gripping her gut.

"Why now?" Juliette whispered to herself, the questions echoing in the quiet room as she fumbled with the bedsheets. The memories were fragments of something she couldn't name, a puzzle with missing pieces that eluded her desperate attempts at understanding. Her nightgown flowed loosely around her as she moved, fumbling over the bed for a sense of solidity. The soft light from outside played through the curtain lace, casting fleeting shadows across the room.

In the solitude of her flat, she spoke to herself and the kitten, voice wavering with vulnerability. "I don't know what it is," she admitted. "But I see moments of it, glimpses. And it makes me want to curl up and hide forever."

But she couldn't do that.

She had a modiste shop to run, things to do. Bow Street captains to not think about.

Her attempts to shake off the remnants of the nightmare proved ultimately futile as she reluctantly swung her legs over the edge of the bed. The morning light filtered through the lace curtains, casting a delicate glow on the room. Determined to face the day, she reached for a simple day dress, the fabric cool and smooth in her trembling hands.

Another visceral memory seized her. The room around her blurred, replaced by the stark memory of hands closing around her, squeezing painfully. A gasp caught in her throat, and she staggered backward, the dress slipping from her hands. Her arms instinctively wrapped around her stomach, a feeble attempt to shield herself from the phantom pain. The small flat, once a haven, felt suddenly constricting, and the air seemed to thicken with the weight of fear.

"*Non,*" she whispered, her voice barely audible in the quiet room. But the ugly memory lingered, an unwelcome intruder that refused to release its grip. Beads of sweat formed on her forehead as fear coiled in the pit of her stomach.

Juliette's eyes darted around the room, seeking refuge from the memories that threatened to overwhelm her. She struggled to steady her breathing, her hands shaking as she clung to the edge of a small vanity. A sense of vulnerability washed over her as she stared at her reflection in the mirror. The woman staring back seemed caught between the present and the haunting past, unsure of where the lines blurred. With a deep, shuddering breath, Juliette fought to regain control over her senses, each inhale a battle against the memories that threatened to drown her.

The dress hung limply from Juliette's trembling fingers as the memory released its grip, leaving her breathless and disoriented. The flat seemed to close in on her, each familiar corner now tainted with the unsettling memories that clawed at her mind.

Helplessness settled over her like a suffocating shroud, and a surge of anger rippled through her. The uncertainty, the gaps in her own history, fueled a deep-seated frustration that gnawed at her very core. "I hate this," she muttered. The woman in the mirror stared back at her, hazel eyes displaying a mix of defiance and vulnerability. The memories, elusive yet haunting, kept her anchored in a past she couldn't fully grasp.

"Not remembering," she whispered, the words a bitter admission. The frustration of being held hostage by fragments of a past she couldn't piece together surged within her. Each memory was a reminder of a life she had lived, yet one that remained shrouded in mystery.

Juliette tried to steady her racing heart, to reclaim a semblance of control. The sunlight offered a fleeting warmth, but the shadows of her own uncertainty persisted.

With a determined breath, Juliette cast aside the remnants of her unsettling morning and focused on the tasks at hand. She put on the modest yet finely crafted day dress, the fabric smooth against her skin. As she descended the narrow staircase from her flat, Odette trailed behind, winding between her legs in an endearing display of morning companionship.

The modiste shop, bathed in the soft glow of morning light, unfolded before Juliette like her own private sanctuary of creativity and craftsmanship. The delicate scent of lavender and the myriad colors of fabrics decorated the space, enveloping the space in tranquility. Around her, antique dummies displayed the latest creations, and ribbons cascaded like waterfalls of color.

Juliette moved with purpose through the shop, her fingers lightly grazing the fabrics and trinkets that spoke of a life she had built with unwavering dedication. She couldn't help but marvel at the beauty of the shop she had created in a mere three years. *"Mon petit paradis,"* she whispered to herself, the words ripe with the pride she felt.

The mornings in her shop, before the hustle and bustle of Bond Street fully awakened, were moments of quiet bliss. The sunlight cast a warm glow on the polished wooden floor— polished to a high sheen with her own two hands. As she reached the counter, a sense of accomplishment filled her. Madame Toussaint's Modiste Shop didn't just display her skills as a seamstress but also her deep-rooted resilience.

However, the very success, the wealth, that had made her life stirred a twinge of worry inside her. And an even bigger twinge of guilt. For what, she knew not. Well, not specifically, at any rate. She only knew that one did not generally lose their life's memories and yet possess enough on-hand wealth in their carpetbag to purchase a small country when they came to consciousness in a dark alley. Not for any innocent reason, anyway.

She looked over the array of hats, dresses, and delicate accessories neatly displayed. The money she had used to purchase the shop, open the business, and make a name for herself lingered as a question mark in her foggy memory. Where had that bag of money come from? The lack of memory surrounding the acquisition of such resources gnawed at her, another puzzle piece missing from the narrative of her life.

"I've built something extraordinary," she mused aloud, her voice echoing in the stillness of the morning. Odette padded over, weaving between the legs of the dummies and chirping softly. "But how did I come by all this? I still can't remember who I was before that night in the alley three summers ago, *mon ami.*"

Despite the peace that blanketed her shop, she couldn't shake the nagging doubts that lurked beneath the surface of her success. As she meticulously arranged fabrics and checked the stitching on a delicate lace overlay, another unsettling thought crept into her mind. "Did the money come from somewhere bad?" she whispered.

Odette, sensing the shift in her demeanor, wound around her ankles again, offering comfort in the face of her uneasy thoughts. Juliette traced the intricate patterns of a silk gown, the material cool against her skin, yet the tendrils of doubt seeped into the very fabric of her existence. Suddenly the success she had built, the modiste shop that stood as her beacon of accomplishment, felt like a fragile house of cards threatening to collapse. She questioned the source of the funds that had allowed her to create this haven. Was it earned through honest means, or did it carry the stain of something darker? Was *she* something darker?

No, she couldn't possibly be.

As she stared at the array of dresses around her, a sense of foreboding lingered. The polished surfaces of the counters and the delicate trinkets on display seemed to hold secrets she couldn't unlock.

With a heavy sigh, she admitted to herself, "I need to know. I can't keep living in the shadows of my own past. I'm going to have to find out where the money came from and who I really, truly am—was?" A flicker of determination ignited in her gut. Odette mewed softly at her feet.

Juliette pushed the front door of the shop open, stepping into the cool embrace of a misty London morning. The air carried a subtle fragrance of damp cobblestones and the distant hint of freshly brewed coffee from a nearby establishment. The mist clung to the elegant façades of the surrounding buildings, casting an almost ethereal aura over the street. The soft murmur of early morning activity echoed through the air as shopkeepers prepared to open their shops for the day. The occasional clip-clop of horse-drawn carriages could be heard, the background rhythm of an awakening Bond Street. Her steps resonated against the damp pavement as she joined the ebb and flow of the city's pulse.

Bond Street, with its cobblestone paths and elegant storefronts, unfolded before her like a canvas of restrained opulence.

High-end boutiques beckoned with their amazing displays, showcasing the latest fashions and accessories. The scent of perfumes wafted through the air, mingling with the damp earthiness of the misty morning. The architecture showcased the city's historical grandeur, the façades adorned with intricate details that spoke of a bygone era. Juliette took in the scene—the polished windows, the gleaming brass signs, and the elaborate ironwork that decorated the lampposts.

As she moved along the street, shopkeepers exchanged morning greetings, their voices a melodic chorus against the backdrop of the awakening city. The scent of fresh bread emanated from a nearby bakery, adding a comforting note to the sensory symphony that enveloped her. The mist, suspended in the air like a whisper-thin veil, lent an otherworldly quality to her surroundings. It clung to her clothes, leaving a refreshing coolness on her skin. The occasional drizzle painted a glistening sheen on the cobblestones, like a reflective, rain-patterned canvas beneath her feet.

With each step, she inhaled the misty London air, hoping to find clarity amidst the fragrances and sounds that defined the city. As she strolled along Bond Street, the mist-kissed morning air embraced her, and the elegant storefronts greeted her with an air of refined allure, urging her to forget her cares. She exchanged nods and smiles with the fellow denizens of the street, punctuated by a few courteous greetings.

"Good morning, Madame Toussaint." A distinguished gentleman tipped his hat, his eyes crinkling in a genial smile.

"Good morning, sir," Juliette replied with a nod, not knowing who he was, but figuring she had clothed a female member of his family.

Further down the street, a group of ladies dressed in fashionable gowns and extravagant hats paused in their animated conversation. "Madame Toussaint, a lovely morning to you," one of the ladies, a vision in a design of lace and silk, said.

Juliette curtsied lightly, her movements graceful and refined.

"Good morning, ladies. I trust you find Bond Street as enchanting as ever."

The morning greetings continued as Juliette made her way down the street, each exchange a choreographed dance of manners and politeness. Such was High Society. Only those of *means* strolled the cobbles of Bond Street in Mayfair.

Just then, a shopkeeper emerged from his establishment, a quaint bookstore overflowing inside with leather-bound volumes and aged parchment. "Madame Toussaint, a pleasure as always," he said, his spectacles perched on the bridge of his nose. "How's your reading list these days? I've a few new tomes that might interest you should you be getting lean on reading material."

Juliette acknowledged him with a gracious smile. "And a good morning to you as well, Mr. Jacobs. I'm well stocked still from our last visit, thank you. May your day be filled with literary delights."

As she continued walking, a sudden chill slithered down her spine, and an ominous weight settled in the pit of her stomach. The genteel atmosphere around her seemed to shatter, replaced by an unsettling awareness that eyes, unseen but undoubtedly present, bored into her. A murmur escaped her lips, a string of muted French words under her breath as a reflexive response to her sudden unease. The hairs on the back of her neck stood at attention, and her eyes darted around, searching for the source of the disquiet that gripped her. *Breathe, Juliette, just breathe.*

Oh, how she hated this panicked feeling that could overwhelm her in moments!

Think and breathe.

The fashionable members of the *ton* continued their amiable exchanges, seemingly unaware of the tension that coiled around Juliette. The mist, once a refreshing companion, now seemed to thicken with an intangible threat. The ambient sounds of the street became muffled, drowned out by the ominous drumming in her ears.

She scanned the faces of the passersby, questioning every

shadow and scrutinizing each corner of the storefronts. The weight of unseen eyes lingered, casting a pall over the graceful ballet of morning greetings. Instinctively, Juliette quickened her pace, the cobblestones beneath her feet echoing with her hurried footsteps. The ominous feeling clung to her, a relentless presence that refused to be shaken off. She resisted the urge to glance over her shoulder; a primal fear gnawed at the edges of her consciousness.

Whose eyes? And where? *Why?*

At the corner of a building across the street, a figure emerged from the murky darkness, and Juliette's breath caught in her throat. The man, a stark contrast to the refined *ton* strolling Bond Street, exuded an air of menace that set her instincts ablaze. He was tall and lean, his body cloaked in a worn and tattered greatcoat that seemed to swallow his form. The fabric, once a deep shade of black, had faded to a sickly gray, bearing the scars of time and neglect. A wide-brimmed hat cast a shadow over his face, concealing features that she strained to discern.

His boots, heavy and scuffed, echoed with a dull thud against the cobblestones as he moved with an unsettling purpose. The collar of his shirt, frayed and disheveled, hinted at a rugged existence. A scar, jagged and ominous, etched a path across one cheek, evidence of a life marked by violence and hardship.

Juliette's gaze locked on to his hands, callused and weather-beaten, fingers that seemed more accustomed to wielding tools of destruction than the delicate fabrics she handled in her shop. A menacing aura enveloped him, an intangible darkness that clung to his every step.

As he glanced in her direction, his eyes met hers from beneath the brim of the hat—piercing orbs that seemed to hold a malevolence that sent a shiver down Juliette's spine. The icy gaze bored into her, devoid of the social niceties that normally defined the interactions on Bond Street.

Her palms instantly grew sweaty, and a wave of fear gripped her. The lovely morning atmosphere evaporated in a puff of smoke, replaced by the primal instinct that warned her of imminent danger. The man across the street, with his rough exterior and haunting presence, seemed like a specter from a nightmare intruding into her perfectly nice morning.

Juliette quickened her pace, her heart pounding. The unease, the near panic, that had gripped her earlier now intensified again, and her instincts screamed in protest. But just as she tried to distance herself from his forbidding presence, a sudden, vivid memory seized her like a vise. The world around her blurred, and the sounds of Bond Street faded into a distant echo. Instead, haunting memories flooded her consciousness, engulfing her in a scene from the past. It replayed in her mind and all around her. "No!" she cried.

She felt the sensation of being grabbed, the pressure on her wrists, and a chilling voice that dripped malevolence. The memory, like a cruel ghost, played out the darkness she desperately sought to suppress. Fear, cold and consuming, gripped her.

The man across the street wasn't just an ominous stranger—he was a direct connection to the darkness that lurked within her own forgotten past. As the fog lifted off that memory, the link between her ever-present fear and the menacing figure crystallized in her mind.

Something *bad* had happened to her.

Juliette, frozen in her tracks, spoke to herself in a voice tinged with fear and, somehow, defiance. "It's… it's all connected," she whispered, the revelation sending shivers down her spine. The morning mist seemed to thicken as she spoke aloud, and the air hung heavy with the weight of the memories she had struggled to unearth. But this one was here in utter clarity.

That man had hurt her.

Her instinct for self-preservation suddenly propelled her into action. Without a second thought, Juliette broke into a run. The peaceful feeling that had surrounded her morning dissipated in the urgency of her sprint. Her heart raced in tandem with her rapid footsteps, and the misty morning air seemed to swirl around her. The shops and boutiques became a mere blur as she dashed past, the haunting figure across the street left behind in her haste.

The echo of her breath, rapid and shallow, mixed with the sounds of Bond Street. Startled gasps and whispers followed in her wake as surprised onlookers tried to make sense of the sudden commotion as she darted past. Driven by a desperate need to escape the man who had somehow hurt her and was connected to her past, Juliette sprinted with a single-minded determination. She maneuvered through the sparse morning crowd, her vision fixed on the destination ahead—the comforting sanctuary of Madame Toussaint's Modiste Shop. The street became a frenzied backdrop to her impromptu flight.

Each stride she made took her closer to the haven she had built for herself, and the sheer physicality of the act provided a momentary distraction from the haunting memories and the ominous figure that had triggered her flight. Bond Street became a fleeting panorama as Juliette raced toward the refuge of familiarity. She needed her things, her space, *now*.

It was all she had.

Her breath hitched and her pulse quickened with each step she took. Yet the haunting figure across the street was no longer her sole focus; now, an image of Captain Catamount Castlebury flashed through her mind and quickly dominated her thoughts.

Juliette suddenly changed direction. Her swift feet carried her in the opposite direction, away from her shop, away from the whispers of her past that lingered in the corners of her memory. The rhythmic echoes of her footsteps reverberated against the grand façades.

As she navigated through the throngs of people, her destination solidified in her mind. The image of Captain Castlebury, with his tawny hair and piercing green eyes, flickered in her thoughts like a guiding beacon. The urgency of reaching the safety of his domain fueled her into a full sprint.

She threaded her way through the labyrinth of streets, her

destination clear in her mind—the Bow Street Runners' head-quarters, where perhaps the answers to the haunting mysteries of her past awaited.

CHAPTER FOUR

CATAMOUNT STOOD IN the lobby of the Runners' headquarters, his broad shoulders filling the space with an air of command. The room itself exuded an air of rugged efficiency, with worn wooden floors and a faint scent of polish lingering in the air.. The walls were lined with maps and notices of wanted criminals, a visual collection of the city's dark underbelly.

Dressed in the uniform of the Runners, Catamount wore a long black coat that accentuated his imposing frame. The polished brass buttons gleamed in the dim light, and a scarlet sash, a mark of his rank, draped diagonally across his chest. His tawny hair, slightly tousled, framed a face marked by the passage of time and the weight of untold burdens.

A few of his men, clad in similarly rugged attire, gathered around him. The clatter of boots on the wooden floor underscored the bustling activity of the headquarters. The flickering light from the gas lamps cast a warm glow, creating pockets of shadow that danced across the room.

"Captain, we've got word that the Revivalists were spotted in Spitalfields again," one of his men reported, spreading a map out on a worn table.

Catamount's eyes narrowed as he absorbed the information. "Spitalfields, again? Blast it. They're like rats, scurrying back to the wreckage."

Another Runner chimed in, his voice gruff. "There's talk on

the streets, baron. The fear's spreading, and folks are getting anxious. We can't keep letting these bastards run rampant."

"We won't. We need to tighten the noose. Get the patrols doubled, and make sure the word is out. We're not letting them slip through our fingers this time."

The men nodded in acknowledgment, dispersing to carry out their orders. Catamount watched them go, a stoic expression on his face. The lobby, with its worn leather furniture and the scent of old parchment, served as the nerve center for the Runners—a place where the battles against crime were planned and executed.

As he paced through the lobby, his gaze fell on a large wanted poster featuring the unknown faces of the Revivalists. The memories of the Seven Dials attack three years ago surged, and a shadow passed over his eyes. The ache in his heart, the loss of Julie, hit him like a hammer. "Find them," he demanded of himself. "Find them before they wreak more havoc."

In the corner of the lobby, a flicker of movement caught his attention. A young Runner approached, saluting smartly. "Baron, there's a woman outside. Looks distressed. Says she needs to speak with you."

Catamount's brow furrowed. "A woman? What does she want?"

The young Runner hesitated before responding. "Says it's about the Revivalists, sir."

Catamount's jaw tightened, and without a word, he strode toward the entrance, his mind already spinning with the possibilities that the woman's words might unravel.

But as he got close to the entrance, the door burst open with an unexpected force, and before he could react, a whirlwind of desperation and fear collided with him. In an instant, he found himself enveloped in the limbs and cloak of a woman who barreled through, her auburn hair a tempest of disarray. Instinct kicked in, and Catamount immediately closed his strong arms around her, absorbing the impact. A palpable undercurrent of fear filled his nostrils as he steadied the woman in his embrace.

"Wait..." he murmured, alarm bells ringing in his head. This woman felt familiar in his arms. *Very* familiar. "Look at me. Look me in the eyes."

She did.

Big, beautiful hazel eyes full of confusion and worry looked directly up at him.

And stopped him in his tracks, sent his heart plummeting to the ground.

They were eyes he knew well.

What in damnation?

"Easy there," Catamount said in a low, calming tone, his hands steady as they supported her, though he didn't feel steady in the least. His heart thundered, and his stomach clenched like a vise. The lobby's usual hum of activity seemed to hush, leaving only the two of them suspended in a charged moment.

The woman blinked up at him, and in that instant, Catamount's world shifted. The vividness of her eyes, the familiarity in their depths—it was like looking into the very soul of someone he had loved and lost. A jolt of confusion and recognition surged through him, making his heart ache with renewed fury.

"Captain, you have to help me," she pleaded, her French-accented voice carrying the urgency of someone teetering on the brink. "I feel like they're watching me—the shadows, the streets. I don't know who, but they're there. And he... he was following me!"

Catamount, still holding her close to his side, guided her further into the lobby, away from the stark exterior. The muted murmurs of his men and the ambient sounds of the headquarters buzzed a steady background around them. "Take a deep breath," he urged.

The woman, catching her breath, began to speak. "I left my shop on Bond Street this morning, and as I was walking, I felt eyes watching me. I turned and saw a man. He... he began to follow me. And I know him, *monsieur*. I do! But I cannot remember from where or when. I only know he is bad. It is all so very terrifying."

As she spoke, Catamount couldn't shake the nagging feeling that her hazel eyes held a familiarity he couldn't ignore. It was as if a ghost from his past had materialized before him, and in her gaze, he saw reflections of someone he had loved and lost.

"I-I did not know where to go, but then I thought of you. And I don't know you, but I knew you would help. I-I don't know why I know that, but I do." As the woman continued to speak, her words shifted into rapid French, a torrent of emotion cascading from her lips. Her hands fluttered in the air, expressing a tumult of feelings that seemed to pour forth in a linguistic dance. The cadence of her voice, the rise and fall of the French syllables, created an intricate melody that filled the lobby.

Catamount, though proficient in French, found himself momentarily captivated by the intensity of her expression. She seemed to find comfort in the fluidity of her native language. He listened, understanding the urgency in her tone even if the intricacies of her words eluded him. Her hands, graceful in their gestures, painted a vivid picture of distress and fear. The moment was filled with confusion and raw emotion.

"*Calmez-vous*," he murmured. "Take a moment and tell me slowly. I will help you. We'll figure this out together."

The woman, wrapped in the whirlwind of her own emotions, kept speaking in rapid French, and Catamount found himself momentarily thrown off guard. The cadence of her words, the fluttering of her hands in the air—all seemed to dissolve the familiar world around him. He suddenly caught her scent again— a fragrance that pierced through the moment like a familiar melody. *Lavender.* The realization struck him with an intensity that tightened his gut with longing.

Julie had smelled like lavender. Lavender from her little potted herb garden.

In that moment, as the woman's words and scent enveloped him, the lobby dipped and swirled and transformed into a surreal landscape. The worn wooden floors and dim lighting seemed to fade into the background, leaving only the Frenchwoman against his side—the woman who looked and smelled like his Julie. Catamount's heart thrummed with a pang of recognition and a surge of emotions he had buried deep within. His Julie, taken from him by the Revivalists, seemed to manifest before him in the hazel-eyed stranger who sought refuge in his embrace.

The world became a haze of confusion and longing as he grappled with the impossibility of the situation. The woman's features mirrored Julie's in a way that defied reason, though she spoke in another language that sounded natural on her tongue. The scent of lavender, a haunting reminder of what he had lost, mingled with the scent of damp cobblestones on the French-woman's skin.

Catamount, caught in his own emotional storm, managed to offer a gentle smile to the woman. *"Permettez-moi de vous trouver une couverture,"* he said. "Let me get you a blanket."

He ushered her into his office, and the worn wooden door creaked softly as he held it open for her. The room, bathed in the muted glow of always-lit gas lamps, felt like a safe retreat from the disorienting waves of familiarity that shook him to his core. "Please, make yourself comfortable." Catamount gestured toward a leather chair. "I'll be right back with that blanket."

As he crossed the room to fetch the blanket from a nearby cabinet, his mind raced with thoughts that defied logic. The woman's presence seemed to unravel the threads of reality. In his heart, a tiny hope resurfaced—a dormant emotion sparked to life by the uncanny resemblance. *What if Julie wasn't dead after all?*

Returning with a folded blanket, Catamount draped it gently over her shoulders. "Here you go," he murmured. "Now, tell me, how can I help you? What has brought you here, to the Bow Street Runners?"

The woman met his gaze. "I don't know, captain. I'm frightened, and I feel like something terrible is happening. When I saw that man following me… I thought maybe you could help."

"I'll do my best. But there's something I have to say first." He studied her face. "You remind me of someone. Someone I lost. It's uncanny."

The woman's brow furrowed. "Lost? I don't understand."

He sighed, running his free hand through his tousled hair. "It's complicated. But there's a familiarity in your eyes, in your presence. It's as if…" He trailed off, unable to articulate the complexity of the emotions swirling within him.

As Catamount settled into the leather chair across from her, the woman met his gaze with a vulnerability that tugged at the edges of his heart. Connection sparked between them. It jarred him hard after so long feeling nothing but sorrow.

"Captain, I don't quite understand it myself," she confessed. "But there was this… pull. When that man started following me and I became scared. When I had these feelings of unease come over me. I felt it then. A call. It was almost overwhelming, like I *needed* to find you. Like you could help me, keep me safe. I don't know how that is possible. I've only ever seen you through the front window of my shop."

His heart skipped a beat. The hollow space within him, where the loss of Julie had left an indelible mark, suddenly seemed to pulse with something unfamiliar. The woman before him wove a tiny thread of hope back into the fabric of his being.

He leaned forward. "I don't fully understand it either," he admitted. "But I'll do everything in my power to help you, to keep you safe. I can't explain this connection either, but I feel it too."

The woman nodded, a flicker of gratitude in her eyes. "Thank you, captain. I know this is all so strange, but I trust that you can help me piece together what's happening."

"Start from the beginning and tell me everything."

"There is not much to tell." She shook her head, her auburn strands swishing about her freckled cheeks. "I saw a man this morning and he began to follow me. His face was familiar, and I don't know how—any more than I understand how I know that you're good and honorable and will help me. But I do know this man is bad in every sense." Her head shook and she frowned as she fluttered her hands in her lap. "I-I have bits of images of him in my mind, hurting me. But I don't remember it clearly or really at all. Only in snippets and in nightmares."

Catamount's blood ran cold. He knew what trauma could do to a person's memory. And this Frenchwoman had just described it perfectly.

Not if he could help it. "Could you identify this man if you were to see him again?" *In a criminal lineup, say.*

A hesitant nod. "*Oui*, I believe so."

His chest tightened with a newfound determination. The office, cast in the soothing glow of the gas lamps, seemed to cocoon them in a space where the mysteries of the past and the uncertainties of the present converged. Sparked. In the hazel-eyed woman, he found a flicker of hope—a chance to unravel the missing part that had haunted him since the day he lost Julie.

"The last three years of my life. That is all I remember." Her quiet voice sliced through the room and commanded his full attention. "I have no memory beyond waking in an alley in Covent Garden near a pub named the Meadowlark Tavern. I know I am French. I know I am a gifted seamstress. That is all I know."

Swallowing hard, Catamount reluctantly removed his hand from where he discovered it stretched across his desk reaching for the Frenchwoman. He hadn't even been aware of doing that! He snatched it back as his mind whirred with questions, the possibility of something unimaginable unfolding before him.

It was utterly impossible.

It was.

Wasn't it?

Catamount looked hard at the woman. Every part inside him lit with recognition and rightness as he assessed her, took her in.

Christ, could it really be her? His Julie, alive and standing before him as this Frenchwoman with no memory? The hazel eyes, the spark of attraction—they were undeniable. But thoughts like that were lunacy, weren't they?

No, it couldn't be her. Julie had died that night in Seven Dials. He knew that. Oh, how he knew that right down to his broken-hearted soul.

Yet…

A flicker of hope, long buried beneath the weight of grief, ignited within him. He wondered in a flash of insight if something had happened that fateful night in Seven Dials, something missed by his men or omitted from the files.

God, what if he *had* truly missed something? Something huge?

His Julie… What if she had survived and been reborn as Juliette with no memory of their shared past? The notion, though utterly ludicrous and incredible, clawed at the edges of possibility. Butted right up snug against it. And it stirred fire within him. As he stared into her eyes, Catamount felt a burning swirl of conflicting emotions—hope, disbelief, grief—and the undeniable pull of a connection that transcended the boundaries of reality and circumstance.

Determined to unearth the truth that lingered in the air un-captured, Catamount felt his resolve harden. "I will do everything in my power to uncover the truth," he declared. His heart, suddenly no longer hollow, pulsed with purpose. He would comb through records, reexamine the files, and piece together the fragments of that night in Seven Dials.

Standing from behind the desk, he began to pace before real-izing in his shock over her appearance he'd forgotten to ask her name. Instantly he spun on the heels of his boots and apologized. "Begging your pardon—I seem to have forgotten to ask your name."

"It's Madame Toussaint," she replied, glancing up at him with stunningly warm and beautiful eyes. "Madame Juliette Toussaint. I own a modiste shop on Bond Street."

Juliette Toussaint.

Her name was Juliette.

Juliette… *Julie.*

His instincts leapt to alert, along with his heart, and he smiled. "Well, Juliette, you were right to come to me."

"Thank you, captain."

The journey into the night began in earnest, and Catamount Castlebury, captain of the Bow Street Runners, would stop at nothing to unveil the mystery of the lovely Juliette and the haunting torment of a past that refused to remain buried.

CHAPTER FIVE

"MADAME TOUSSAINT," CAPTAIN Castlebury began, fixing his eyes on hers from across the office with an intensity that made her uneasy. "You've shared your story, but there's something you're not telling me. Something you fear. I can sense it."

Juliette hesitated. Of course she did. How could she explain what she herself didn't understand? She couldn't, so she settled for half-truth. "Captain, it's the Revivalists. The mere mention of them sends a chill down my spine. They are ruthless, and their return... It terrifies me. I fear for my safety and the safety of those around me. And I fear that this man who followed me may somehow be connected to them."

Castlebury leaned forward, resting his arms on the desk. "You mentioned feeling a pull, a call to find me. Why, Madame Toussaint? What connection do you think we have?"

The question hung in the air, and Juliette felt a twinge of vulnerability. "I don't know, captain. It's inexplicable. But you... you seem familiar, like I should know you. Have we met before?"

Castlebury's gaze lingered on her face. "I can't shake the feeling that I know you too, like I said earlier. Your eyes, the way you move... It's as if you hold a piece of my past."

Juliette's pulse quickened, uncertainty clouding her thoughts. "I assure you, captain, I am just a modiste from France. I hold no pieces to anything. Nor do I have any secrets that could be of importance to you or anyone else."

He continued to watch her, a furrow forming between his brows. "There's more to this, Madame Toussaint. I can feel it. Tell me the truth. What is it that you're not saying?"

A moment of silence lingered before she finally spoke. "I don't remember my life beyond three years ago."

"You mentioned that."

"But it's all a haze, captain. You don't understand! I start each morning with no recollection of who I was before waking up in that alley. And the flashes... the fear! I can't explain it. All of it taunts me cruelly."

Castlebury's eyes softened. "Flashes? In your mind? What do you see?"

Juliette went quiet and thought long and seriously about what—and how much—to share. Taking a deep, fortifying breath, she glanced into his green eyes and then recounted the snippets of darkness, fear, and blood that haunted her. "I see glimpses, but they're fragmented. I don't know what they mean or where they come from. And the unease, the fear... It's always there, lurking. Men laughing horribly, glass shattering, the smell of fire and smoke."

The captain sat and leaned back in his chair, his gaze narrowing to a piercing intensity. Those liquid green eyes locked on to hers, and Juliette felt a tug deep in her belly. The weight of his scrutiny seemed to unravel layers of her that she didn't know she had, exposing vulnerabilities she hadn't anticipated.

"Madame Toussaint," he said, "there's something more here that I can sense, that my Bow Street instincts alert me to. Whatever connection you feel that binds us goes beyond the man who followed you today and your fear of the Revivalists. Tell me, do you truly remember nothing before three years ago? Perhaps another tavern in another part of London? Say... Seven Dials?"

Juliette swallowed hard, her palms instantly going damp at the name, but she emphatically shook her head. "Captain, I swear to you, my memory is a blank canvas beyond that point. It's as if my life began the moment I woke up in that alley, speaking French, and surrounded by unfamiliar faces, but in possession of a modiste shop that apparently belonged to me." *That* truth she skirted around. She'd never told a soul about the bag of money she'd possessed when she awoke in that alley—and as much as she felt drawn to Captain Castlebury, she would keep that information private for now.

"Juliette, these flashes you speak of… They might hold the key. We need to uncover the truth, for both our sakes. When you're ready, you'll confide in me."

As he spoke, Juliette couldn't ignore the magnetic pull, the strange familiarity that lingered in the air. She shifted her gaze away from his penetrating stare, allowing herself a moment to take in the details of his office. The leather chair she occupied, the soft blanket over her shoulders, the flickering gas lamps casting shadows on the walls, and the subtle scent of old paper—all seemed to suit the man perfectly.

She inhaled deeply, steadying herself, and then decided to redirect the conversation.

"Captain," she began, "this office of yours—it holds the air of a man deeply entrenched in his duty. It makes me wonder about the items that surround you. What's the story behind that weathered map on the wall? And the worn-out book there, on the corner of your desk? They must hold tales of a life well lived."

Castlebury followed her gaze to the map and the book, then offered a small, almost rueful smile. "The map is a relic from my early days with the Runners—a reminder of the streets I swore to protect. It's marked with the boundary of my first official patrol route. The book is a gift from my brother, Crawford. It's a volume of Shakespeare, weathered but cherished. Something to cling to in the hard moments."

As he spoke, Juliette noted the weariness etched on his handsome face. Lines of experience and perhaps a touch of cynicism shadowed his features. She couldn't help but be drawn to the vulnerability beneath the façade of strength. "Captain," she continued, attempting to keep the conversation moving, "how do you manage the weight of the city on your shoulders? It must be exhausting, yet you seem resolute."

Castlebury smirked, his eyes glinting with a knowing amusement. Juliette's attempt to shift his focus clearly hadn't gone unnoticed. "Well, madame," he began, "I suppose managing the city's burdens comes with the territory. It's not a task for the faint of heart, but it keeps me on my toes. Now, since you're so keen on the stories in this room, what tales do you think these walls hold?"

Juliette breathed in relief, feeling a bit of tension ease from her shoulders. "Oh, captain, I imagine there are countless stories hidden within these walls. Stories of triumph, heartache, and perhaps a touch of scandal. The kind of tales that linger, like the echoes of footsteps in an empty street. Harlots and bandits and madmen."

Catamount's smirk softened into a genuine smile. "You have a poetic way of looking at things. But perhaps you're onto something. Every corner of this city has a story to tell, and as a Runner, I aim to uncover those tales and bring justice to the forefront."

As they bantered about the stories within the office, she couldn't get over the feeling that there was more to Catamount's gaze, a familiarity that danced at the edges of her memory. Like she knew it, that intense green gaze of his, intimately. But how could that be?

Juliette's mind was suddenly invaded by an intense, vivid flash. A memory—or a figment of her imagination—of a hard, unforgiving mouth pressed against hers, kissing her senseless. The image left her breathless, her heart racing. And that demanding mouth belonged to the Bow Street captain sitting across from her.

Her gaze shot back to Captain Castlebury, who, in that moment, seemed to have an uncanny awareness of the turmoil within her. The unspoken connection between them crackled in the air, leaving Juliette feeling exposed, as if he could unravel the secrets locked within her mind.

She couldn't help but notice the way his muscles flexed beneath the fabric of his jacket. Averting her eyes, she inhaled deeply, absorbing the subtle scent of leather and ink that enveloped the room.

Trying to dispel the escalating tension, Juliette shifted her focus to the worn leather chair across from her, as if it held the answers she sought. "And what about this chair, captain? It looks like it has a tale or two to tell."

He followed her gaze, a faint smile playing on his lips. "This old thing has been witness to many a late-night deliberation and a fair share of contemplation. It's comfortable, if nothing else."

Juliette raised an eyebrow. "Contemplation, you say? What thoughts trouble the mind of a seasoned Runner, I wonder?"

Catamount's expression grew thoughtful. "The past has a way of lingering, Miss Toussaint. It leaves its mark, and sometimes, no amount of running, Bow Street or otherwise, can escape it."

Sensing the weight of his unspoken sorrows, she hesitated for a moment before pressing on. "And yet here you are, facing those shadows head-on. I'd say it takes a special kind of strength."

His gaze met hers, the green depths revealing a mixture of resilience and vulnerability. "Strength is a necessity in this line of work, but it doesn't make one immune to the echoes of the past."

"Perhaps," she mused, "sometimes it takes more strength to confront those echoes than to chase new mysteries."

As he leaned forward, Juliette couldn't help but feel a flutter in her belly. His voice, only a moment ago composed and professional, dipped into a warm and intimate register. "Julie," he murmured, the name slipping from his lips like a caress. The unexpected familiarity of the name caught Juliette off guard, sending a heated shiver down her spine. A charged silence hung in the air, and he gazed at her with a depth of recognition that bordered on unsettling. "Julie," he repeated, his voice laden with tenderness and longing.

Grappling with a sudden, wholly unexpected surge of emotions, Juliette found herself torn between a desire to lean into the intimacy of the moment and the need to correct him and assert her own identity. She drew a steadying breath. "Captain, it's Juliette," she said. "Not Julie. Juliette."

Taking a moment, she carefully removed and folded the captain's blanket, leaning forward to set it on his desk, her hand lingering on the still-warm fabric. As she rose from her seat, the folds of her elegant rose silk dress cascaded around her in a soft, fluid dance. The material clung to her in alluring simplicity, accentuating her curves with a subtle grace. A delicate lace hem skimmed the edges, adding a touch of refined femininity.

His gaze lingered on her, his eyes tracing the lines of her silhouette with an intensity that went beyond the usual scrutiny. Something unspoken passed behind his eyes. Something hot and hungry and haunted.

She met his gaze. "Good day, captain," she said, her voice steady despite the shaking in her core.

With that, she turned and left his office, feeling the weight of his intense, lingering gaze trailing after her.

"Good day, Julie."

Juliette's steps faltered for a moment at the door upon her hearing that familiar yet misplaced name. "Juliette," she corrected him again without glancing over her shoulder.

With that, she swept down the corridor and left behind the enigmatic captain with his liquid green eyes and the nagging feeling that they were somehow connected.

CHAPTER SIX

A S THE FRENCHWOMAN named Juliette exited Catamount's office, he wasted no time. He rolled up the sleeves of his crisp linen shirt and called out, "Lieutenant Harcourt, bring me everything we have on the Revivalists. Specifically, I want all the files related to their attack on Seven Dials three years ago that I don't already have. Scrape the barrel and find me something!"

As Harcourt hurried to gather the requested files, Catamount's gaze drifted to the large window overlooking the bustling streets of London below. His jaw clenched with determination, and he could feel the weight of responsibility settling on his shoulders. The Revivalists had haunted his thoughts for years, and now, with Juliette's unexpected appearance, the past and present intertwined in a way he'd never anticipated.

The lieutenant returned promptly, a stack of files in hand, and placed them on Catamount's desk. Wasting no time, he delved into the documents, scanning through reports, witness statements, and any shred of information related to the attack. The flickering lamplight cast shadows on his face as he absorbed the details, his mind racing to connect the dots.

The memories of that tragic night, the loss of Julie, fueled his determination to unravel the mysteries surrounding the Revivalists. As Catamount delved into the past, he couldn't shake the feeling that Juliette's presence held the key to unlocking the truth of that night—one that had eluded him for far too long. But he had to be careful. He didn't want to scare her away. Not now. Not when he'd only just found her.

With each page he turned, the echoes of that night reverberated through his mind. The clock on the wall ticked away, marking the passage of time as he embarked on a relentless pursuit of justice and closure. He just knew the truth lay buried within the pages before him, waiting to be unveiled. As he scrutinized the details, Harcourt stood at attention, ready to assist, his brown eyes direct and confident.

Catamount traced the lines of the documents. "Harcourt, what do you remember about that night? The night the Revivalists attacked Seven Dials," he asked, his voice steady, betraying little emotion.

The lieutenant rubbed his chin thoughtfully. "It was terrible, captain. A bloody mess. The Revivalists hit the tavern where your woman, Julie Burness, worked—the Black Griffin—before taking to the streets. Bodies everywhere. The whole damn Seven Dials nearly burned to the ground."

Catamount's jaw clenched at the mention of the tavern where Julie had worked and where everything had unraveled. But he'd asked. He should have been prepared. "Body counts? Damage to the building?"

Harcourt consulted his own notes. "Twenty-four casualties, sir. Most civilians. The Black Griffin was left in ruins, and the surrounding structures suffered damage from the fire. We rounded up a few clues about the direction they'd gone, but the Revivalists had vanished by the time we arrived."

Catamount sighed. "Julie..." he whispered. They'd found her ring—the one he'd given to her when he'd proposed the week before, his family's protests be damned—next to an unidentifiable female body, and he'd known. That night he'd lost his heart.

"Captain, we did our best that night, but the Revivalists were elusive. No one expected them to strike with such brutality," Harcourt said. "Or so quickly."

Catamount nodded, his gaze fixed on the reports. "We underestimated them, and it cost us. We thought they were done, but they've resurfaced. And now, with this woman—Juliette—claiming a connection to that night, I need to know more."

Harcourt leaned against the desk. "You think she might have answers, sir?"

Catamount met his lieutenant's gaze. "I don't know what to think, but I can't ignore the possibility. We owe it to the victims of that night to uncover the truth, even if it means confronting the ghosts we thought were laid to rest."

As he continued to scrutinize the reports, a nagging suspicion burrowed into the recesses of his mind. Juliette seemed more than she appeared. The resemblance to Julie was uncanny, save for the French lilt that danced in her words. Yet her hazel eyes regarded him without a flicker of recognition. None. Nothing.

It was hell.

Agony and hope churned in Catamount's chest, and his heart—a vessel that had seemingly died with Julie—thumped with renewed intensity. The past, with its scars and unanswered questions, had resurfaced with Juliette's presence.

He sighed, the weight of it all pressing down on him. "Harcourt, gather any remaining reports, witness accounts, and sketches from that night. I need to know if there's anything I missed, anything at all that might connect this woman to the Revivalists or to Julie."

The lieutenant nodded. "Other than the fact that she looks exactly like her, you mean."

Catamount paused, his gaze fixed on the parchment before him. "Down to the freckle pattern on her nose. Still, I don't know what to think. There's something about her, that's for damn certain. Something familiar, yet elusive. I promise you this, Harcourt: if Julie somehow survived that night, if she's living today as the lovely Madame Juliette Toussaint with no memory of our past together, I need to find out."

"Anyone would, captain. Getting a second chance with a lost

loved one doesn't come along every day."

No, it certainly did not.

Harcourt left to gather the requested materials, leaving Catamount alone with his thoughts. The dim light cast shadows on his furrowed brow as he grappled with the inexplicable connection between Julie, Juliette, and the Revivalists.

Catamount couldn't contain the frustration building within him, and a low curse escaped his lips. "Damn it," he muttered to himself. His tumultuous emotions refused to be silenced. Agitated, he grabbed his coat and bellowed for his lieutenant once again, signaling his abrupt departure from the confines of headquarters. "Take over, Harcourt!"

His destination was Flatt's boxing gym. In the hope of finding some reprieve from the pressure gripping his chest like an unrelenting vise, he thought of Aaron Longfellow, the bareknuckle champion and gym owner, and his brother-in-law, Damon Crowe. Christ, he couldn't wait to punch them in the face.

CATAMOUNT STEPPED INTO the gym, the scent of sweat and leather hitting him like a familiar slap. The large, open building with its brick walls echoed with the sounds of exertion and the rhythmic thud of fists meeting punching bags. Grunts and expletives and flesh on flesh. The physical energy of the place enveloped him. He scanned the diverse crowd, a mix of fighters honing their skills and spectators absorbing the raw intensity of the gym. Amid the sea of bodies, he spotted the imposing figure of Longfellow, the giant auburn-haired boxer.

With a determined stride, Catamount approached him. "Longfellow, mind if I join you for a spar? I could use the exertion."

Longfellow, always up for a challenge, flashed a knowing

grin. "Catamount, me bloke, you're always welcome in my ring. I'll clean the mat wit' ye."

Catamount laughed, ready and eager for the match. "Try it, Longfellow. You might just succeed, but not for my lack of effort." Grabbing his jacket, he shed his clothes until he was bare-chested. Riding low, his trousers settled loosely about his lean hips as he climbed into the ring.

The two men circled each other between the ropes, the air charged with the promise of an intense match. Catamount, despite his own physical prowess, recognized Longfellow's reputation as a formidable champion. The rhythmic dance of their footwork echoed through the gym as they sized each other up.

"Anytime now, detective."

"I'm assessing," Catamount retorted, searching for an opening.

Suddenly Longfellow's powerful frame moved with a deceptive agility, his muscles rippling beneath the sheen of sweat. In a burst of speed, he closed the distance, launching a lightning-fast combination. Catamount, no stranger to combat, deftly dodged and blocked the initial strikes. But Longfellow's precision was undeniable. A quick feint drew Catamount off balance, and with a thunderous hook, the bare-knuckled champion clipped him hard on the jaw. The impact sent shock waves through his skull, and he stumbled backward, the taste of copper filling his mouth.

The gym fell silent for a moment as Catamount found himself flat on his arse on the canvas, his senses momentarily scattered. Longfellow, displaying a wide, satisfied grin of victory, offered a hand to help him up. "Not too bad, cap'n."

As Catamount took it and dragged himself up from the canvas, he grinned and flinched at the split in his lip. "Damn, Longfellow, you've still got those lightning fists. Should've known better than to let my guard down."

The boxer chuckled. "You're not as rusty as ye pretend, Catamount. Just needed a reminder, tha's all."

Catamount wiped a bead of sweat from his brow, the physical exertion providing a temporary escape from the tangled thoughts that swirled in his mind. "Well, you certainly delivered that reminder with panache. Let's go another round. I want another chance to best you."

They resumed their sparring, the sounds of bare fists meeting flesh and the occasional grunt filling the gym. Catamount, fueled by the need to vent his frustration and the lingering ache of memories, threw himself into this match with renewed determination. He landed a solid jab, feeling the satisfying thud as his hand connected with Longfellow's midsection.

Longfellow grimaced before his sweat-slicked face broke into a good-natured smile. "Tha's the idea, cap'n. Keep me on my toes."

As they circled each other, Catamount's gaze sharpened with a sudden realization. He stopped and stared at Longfellow, pieces clicking into place. "You know, that blow you sent me almost made me forget my own damn name."

Longfellow arched an eyebrow. "Is tha' so?"

"Yes, and it got me thinking. What if… what if something like that happened to her? What if she forgot that night, and is really my Julie?"

Longfellow paused mid-step, his jovial demeanor giving way to a more serious look. "Julie? You mean the one you lost in the Seven Dials attack?"

Catamount's mind raced, connecting the dots with the force of a revelation. "She doesn't remember," he muttered, more to himself than to Longfellow. "But the way she looks at me, the way she feels so familiar… What if she's really, truly my Julie, and something awful happened that night, something she can't recall but survived? Shite, it's got to be her and she just doesn't *remember.*"

"I'm bloody uncertain wot nonsense you're spoutin' about Julie. It's a strange notion, eh? Her still being alive but without her memory. And bloomin' unlikely."

Catamount clenched his jaw. "I'll get to the bottom of it, Longfellow. Watch me."

The possibility of reclaiming something he'd thought forever gone?

Yes. Absolutely bloody fucking *yes*.

CHAPTER SEVEN

JULIETTE DEFTLY HANDLED the rich, silken fabric, her latest arrival from Paris destined for a Society lady's evening gown. Her fingers moved with practiced grace, sewing and shaping the material as she engaged in light chatter with her customers. The modiste shop bustled with the hushed excitement of women seeking the latest fashion trends, discussing fabrics, lace, and the intricate details that made their garments unique. As well as men. Always the men. And scandals. Oh, the love they possessed for a good scandal.

"Madame Toussaint, do you think this shade of blue will complement my eyes?" inquired Viscountess Darlow, a regular client with discerning tastes.

Juliette studied the fabric in question and then looked up, a warm smile playing on her lips. "*Oui.* Absolutely, Lady Amelia. That particular shade will accentuate the beauty of your eyes and add a touch of elegance to the gown. Brilliant choice."

The ladies chatted animatedly about the upcoming social events—though there were dismally few, it being past the height of the Season—their talk seamlessly transitioning between the newest fabrics and the latest gossip.

Juliette's mind, however, kept wandering back to Captain Catamount Castlebury.

She recalled the warmth in his gaze from the other day, the way he looked at her as if searching for something elusive, something deeply personal. The memory of his muscular frame and those piercing green eyes lingered, interrupting her ability to focus on the fashion discussions.

"Madame Toussaint, what do you think of this lace for my daughter's wedding dress?" asked Mrs. Langley from across the room, presenting a delicate piece of lace for her inspection.

Juliette examined the material from afar. "Ah, exquisite choice, Mrs. Langley. It will add a touch of sophistication and romance to her dress. Your daughter will be radiant. Set that with your other selections and I'll make certain it is added to your purchase."

Was Catamount Castlebury merely a dashing officer of the law, or did their connection really run deeper, stemming from a past she struggled to remember?

Blast, how was it that she really couldn't remember her life beyond that Covent Garden alley?

Really, who did that *actually* happen to?

Losing one's memory in a woosh! Gone! Life—erased. Like a cheap novel character.

Only she wasn't a fictional character, and it was the truth of her life whether she liked it or not.

Juliette's nimble fingers continued their dance with the fabric as she fitted the viscountess, yet her mind kept snaring on the memory of the Bow Street captain. The ruggedness of his jawline and the hint of bronze stubble added a certain virility that stirred unexpected feelings within her, made her fingers itch to touch its velvet roughness, as if they knew the feel of his day's facial hair growth. Her cheeks warmed with a blush, the realization of her wayward thoughts catching her off guard.

Focus, Juliette!

She needed to tend the task at hand, guiding her customers through the selection of fabrics and styles, but the captain had left an indelible mark on her thoughts, apparently. Like she were an infatuated fool.

As she continued to assist her customers, a vivid, impossible vision of his mouth pressed urgently against hers invaded her thoughts, stole her breath. She gasped at the flash in her mind, like an unexpected gust of wind, stirring a whirlwind of sensations within her. The heat of his kiss, demanding and fervent, swept through her mind, a tantalizing echo of an encounter she couldn't fully comprehend and knew hadn't happened. Certainly not in the past three years. But she *felt* it. Exactly like it had happened. Really, truly happened. Like a moment burned into her memory.

"Qu'est-ce qui se passe?" she whispered as her mind swirled with vignettes of an intimate moment with the captain that had never been. How could this be?

Juliette's fingers stilled on the delicate fabric, the mental image of an intense kiss with Castlebury replaying like a sweet, haunting melody. The modiste shop faded into the background of her consciousness as she tumbled into the private realm of her own thoughts. The impossible flash of memory carried with it desire, familiarity, and confusion—a potent cocktail that left her momentarily shaken and disoriented.

Of course, she questioned the origin of such vivid memories, the validity of them, especially when the man starring in them seemed like a stranger. Yet the undeniable pull of those sensations, the way his hard, commanding lips had left an indelible mark on her consciousness, refused to be dismissed. What was truth—and was her mind playing cruel tricks on her?

"Did you hear about the Revivalist attack in Shoreditch last night?" one of the ladies exclaimed suddenly, jarring her from her visions.

Juliette discreetly turned her attention to the conversation, alarm piqued. A group of ladies near the German lace rack huddled together, sharing the latest horrible, scandalous details.

"The *Gazette* printed this morning that the Revivalists struck minutes before midnight, causing panic in the streets as they wrecked one establishment after another, and burned a haberdashery to the ground," another lady chimed in. "They're becoming more daring, more frequent in their attacks, I say."

"Three found dead, reported the *Daily News*."

Lady Amelia gasped, clutching her fan in front of her face. "Oh, the poor people of Shoreditch! What is the world coming to? These attacks are getting out of hand!"

Juliette subtly continued working while eavesdropping on the ladies' gossip, her stomach churning greasily. The vivid descriptions of the destruction in Shoreditch painted a stark contrast to the refined atmosphere of her shop. Terror against comfort and safety.

As the ladies continued their animated discussion, a new fear began to creep up Juliette's spine. The talk of the group that haunted her nightmares triggered a heaviness in her chest. A dark shadow seemed to encroach upon the corners of her mind, pushing at her, and she fought the instinct to let that fear take hold. She busied her hands with fabrics and threads, attempting to drown out the awful whispers of an unclear past.

"How are you enjoying this unseasonably warm autumn day?" she asked loudly, trying to divert the conversation.

No such fortune. The ladies doggedly kept on their topic of choice.

The bell above the door chimed, announcing the entrance of a customer. Juliette looked up, and her breath caught in her throat as Captain Castlebury stepped inside. His ruggedly virile figure, with his tawny hair tousled in a way that only added to his appeal, seemed strikingly out of place amidst the delicate fabrics and femininity of the shop.

In his long coat and trousers that emphasized his athletic build, Castlebury exuded a raw, masculine energy that drew the attention of every lady in the room.

Startled by his unexpected appearance, Juliette quickly scanned the shop, ensuring that her other customers were engrossed in their own conversations. They were not. They were as enamored with his presence as she was. Ninnies, the lot of them. Herself included.

With a forced smile, she approached him. "Captain Castlebury, what a surprise to see you here," she greeted him, attempting to maintain an air of casual politeness. "To what do I owe the pleasure of a visit from the Bow Street Runners in my humble establishment?" Her words flowed smoothly, but beneath the polite façade, a current of tension built.

Castlebury's gaze lingered on her, his eyes probing as if searching for something deeper within her. "Madame Toussaint," he said, his voice a low rumble that sent a shiver down her spine, "I was hoping we could continue our conversation from the other day. I've been thinking about it quite a bit."

She nodded. "Of course, captain. How can I assist you?"

His lips curved into a faint smile. "Perhaps somewhere more private? I have some questions I'd like to discuss with you."

The unease intensified in Juliette's chest, but she managed to maintain her composed exterior. "Certainly, captain. Follow me to my office," she suggested, leading him to the small, secluded room at the back.

Once inside, he closed the door behind them, and the sounds of the shop faded away. "Juliette," he began, his gaze never wavering from hers, "there's something about you that feels... familiar. I know I said it already. Many times, in fact. But I can't quite put my finger on it, and it's there, taunting me. With your loss of memory... and with the timing of it and when I lost her... I believe you might be someone who was very important to me."

Her heart quickened, and she fought to maintain her composure. Why did such a notion make her yearn so desperately? "Captain, I assure you, I'm just a modiste trying to make a living. I don't see how I could be familiar to someone like you. We literally have never met before I stepped into the Bow Street Runners' headquarters the other day."

Castlebury leaned against the edge of her cluttered desk. "Julie," he murmured, a trace of uncertainty in his voice.

She tensed at the use of that name. Why, she wasn't sure. But it irked her just the same. "It's Juliette, captain. And I believe you may be mistaken."

His expression tightened, as if he were grappling with conflicting thoughts. "Forgive me if I'm pushing. It's just... something about you seems too familiar to dismiss. Your presence is exactly like a woman named Julie Burness. It's utterly uncanny."

Icy tendrils ran down Juliette's spine, and she struggled to maintain a façade of nonchalance. "Captain, I'm just a Frenchwoman trying to navigate London Society to ply my trade. I don't possess any hidden mysteries. At this point, honestly, I wish I did. Any memories beyond three years ago would be most welcome. Alas, I cannot help you."

He studied her for a moment longer before relenting with a nod. "Very well. Perhaps it's just my mind playing tricks on me. But if you remember or sense anything unusual, anything that might connect you to anything beyond three years ago, I implore you to talk to me. It could be crucial for both of us."

With those words, the captain left her office, leaving Juliette alone with the lingering weight of unspoken truths and a growing unease about the mysteries that seemed to entwine their fates.

Suddenly, the door swung back open. Juliette looked up, her heart racing, and there he was once more, his gold-tipped hair slightly disheveled, an apology on his lips and a storm in his green eyes. "Juliette, I'm sorry," he muttered. Without waiting for a response, he closed the distance between them in quick, powerful strides. "I have to know."

Before she could utter a word, he pulled her into his strong arms, his apology giving way to a deep, possessive kiss. Time seemed to stand still as the world outside faded away, leaving only the warmth of his lips on hers, the strength of his embrace, and the unspoken emotions that crackled between them.

As his lips pressed against hers, Juliette felt a rush of sensations—his large and commanding presence, the heat that emanated from him, and the undeniable chemistry that pulsed between them. Lost in the moment, she allowed herself to be enveloped by the strength of his embrace, the world outside the shop fading into insignificance. She fell wantonly into his kiss, a fusion of longing and discovery, a magnetic pull that defied explanation. Her hands instinctively found their way to his broad, sculpted chest, feeling the steady beat of his heart beneath the fabric of his coat. His lips moved with a fervent urgency, as if seeking confirmation of something only he could know, and she responded with open surrender and flaring desire.

For that suspended moment, the past and present converged, and all that remained was the shared breaths, the rhythmic beating of their hearts, and the intangible feeling of a connection that seemed to transcend time and circumstance. The sensation of his lips on hers mingled with those elusive visions that had assailed her earlier. It felt… exactly the same. Exactly *right*.

So incredibly familiar.

Juliette melted against him. The heat of his kiss, the demand of his lips, coupled with the hardness of his large body, stirred something within her—a fusion of desire and confusion and elusive memory that left her dizzy.

As her lips left his, a quiet settled between them, the weight of unspoken questions lingering in the air. Juliette's eyes met his, and for a fleeting moment, his liquid green gaze filled with recognition and an inexplicable longing.

He uttered softly, "Julie."

No.

"You have to be her."

But she wasn't. He wanted somebody else. Not her.

She gracefully stepped from his embrace. "I'm Juliette," she stated quietly. For as long as she could remember.

Inclining her head, she left him standing alone in her office, a whirlwind of emotions in his eyes.

CHAPTER EIGHT

HARCOURT POUNDED ON Catamount's office door later that afternoon before striding through. "We've a lead, captain, found in an old journal discarded in a rubbish bin outside Lord Arnold's theatre the night he killed himself. You know, from when he took your sister."

Catamount's gaze shot up from where he'd been reading the daily report, every part of him tensing, alert. "Tell me."

"We think it may be an itinerary of sorts. Or perhaps a map. Or both. We're not certain. But it's hand-drawn locations around London with circles around them, and they're numbered. The first attack location in Spitalfields is marked with the number one, and they seem to line up sequentially as they've happened recently. Given that, Michaelson believes he's deciphered a location and date for the next attack—and it's today."

Catamount leapt from his seat behind his desk, his heart thumping. "What are we waiting for? Give me details on the way."

"Yes, captain."

IN THE NARROW, winding streets of St. Giles, Catamount led his party with determined strides. The flickering gas lamps cast sporadic pools of light, revealing the worn cobblestones and the shadows lurking in the corners. His companions, his brother Crawford, Rainville, Duke of Somerton, and Damon Crowe, Viscount Amslee, followed closely. Harcourt had taken a team of Runners in the opposite direction to cover more territory.

Catamount scanned the decrepit buildings that leaned precariously, like old men bowing under the weight of time. The air was thick with the scent of decay and desperation. Despite the darkness, the group pressed on, footsteps echoing through the labyrinthine alleys.

Crawford spoke up. "Any idea where we should start, Cat?"

"We're looking for any signs of Revivalist activity. According to the journal Harcourt found, they should be here tonight. Spread out, check every corner, every nook."

As they ventured deeper into St. Giles, the glow from the gas lamps grew dimmer. Catamount could feel the weight of the Revivalists on his shoulders—the memories of that night in Seven Dials. The poverty-stricken St. Giles air seemed to carry the echoes of pain and violence that had scarred this part of London.

Rainville nodded to Damon. "Spread out. Look for any suspicious gatherings or hideouts. We need to find them before they strike again. Any man in black is suspect."

Damon, ever ready, nodded. The group moved like a well-trained unit, eyes sharp and senses alert to the slightest hint of danger. The dark alleys whispered with secrets, and Catamount knew in his gut that they were being watched. Hairs on the back of his neck rose, alerting him.

The crumbling façades of buildings loomed over them, their once-grand architecture now reduced to dilapidated silhouettes against the night sky.

Lost in thought, Catamount muttered to himself, "If they're here, we'll find them. We have to."

They pushed on, and the footsteps of his group echoed through the eerie silence, punctuated only by distant sounds from the Docklands. The night seemed to hold its breath as they sought the elusive trail of the Revivalists.

Catamount, his gaze fixed on the sad surroundings, said in a measured tone, "I've got a potential lead, Crawford. Someone came to me, someone who might have a connection to the Revivalists. I can't ignore the feeling that they're gearing up for something big."

Crawford raised an eyebrow, sensing the weight behind his brother's words. "Who is this person? How can you be sure they're not leading you into a trap?"

Catamount's jaw clenched, the image of the mysterious Juliette mingling with his resolve. "I don't know yet. But there's something about her, and I intend to find out exactly what it is. She looks exactly like Julie, and came to me in fear of the Revivalists. One man in particular. It's like she's connected to my past, to Julie. Perhaps it even *is* Julie."

Rainville exchanged a glance with Damon. "Um, Julie died three years ago, Cat."

"But what if she didn't?" Catamount shot back, knowing they wouldn't understand. Not until they saw Juliette for themselves. Then they'd see what he saw.

Rainville said, "If there's even a chance she survived, and that they're planning the big one, we can't afford to wait. We strike now, while we have the opportunity. So let's find these bastards."

Damon, ever pragmatic, added, "But we need to proceed with caution. We don't want to tip our hand too soon. We follow them, but we stay vigilant."

Catamount nodded in agreement. "We press on. We find them before they strike again, and we put an end to this once and for all."

The group continued through the winding, narrow alleys of St. Giles, each step a silent declaration of their resolve to protect the city from the looming threat of the Revivalists. The night enveloped them, the air thick with anticipation, as they ventured deeper into the heart of darkness in pursuit of justice.

"Let's go over potential suspects within the nobility," Crawford said in a hushed voice as he walked along.

Rainville voiced his suspicions: "It could be someone with a grudge against the Crown, perhaps an aristocrat who feels slighted or seeks revenge for some perceived wrong. Like Lord Ballingwood. His attempt to pass legislation in the House of Lords failed dismally last session."

Damon, with a calculating glint in his eyes, said, "Or it might be someone with an ideological agenda. The Revivalists have shown a willingness to use violence to advance their cause. Perhaps it's a radical with a vendetta against the current establishment. The Revivalists believe themselves to be traditionalists. Progress of any kind could be call to violence for them. Look to toffs like Earl Warbleton. He's a supporter of renewing the medieval serf system, and thinks the chastity belt for ladies is dismally underutilized."

"More like extinct," retorted Rainville.

"Not in Warbleton's warped mind they're not," Damon pointed out.

Catamount listened attentively but remained silent, his gaze focused on the dimly lit alleys ahead.

Crawford, noting his restraint, nudged him lightly. "Any thoughts, brother? You're being unusually quiet."

"I'll refrain from speculation until we have concrete evidence," Catamount replied. "Let's focus on finding the Revivalists first. Motives can come later."

"But I'm not done yet," Damon said with a sharp grin. "I've got years of information like this stored up inside me. Comes with my glamorous job. Lord Harrington has a reputation for ruthless eviction of tenants in the Docklands. He'd have a slew of enemies, especially after what happened with the protests against him last year. A sod like him would take that pressure out on somebody else."

In his line of private recovery work for the rich and titled, Damon knew of which he spoke.

Rainville agreed and added a name to the list. "What about Lord Drayton? His financial schemes have ruined countless businesses, pushing honest folks to destitution. The Revivalists might see him as a symbol of upholding balance within the aristocracy."

Crawford chimed in, "And we can't forget Lord Istan Stanton. He's been accused recently of using his influence to manipulate legal proceedings to push new-monied gentry off their lands. There's enough resentment against him to fuel a rebellion. The Revivalists would see him as an aristocratic hero, a preserver of traditional bloodlines and landholdings."

Catamount interjected finally with a thoughtful observation: "I've been giving thought lately to the notion that the Revivalists might be hiding behind a woman. One of wealth and status. We know it's a fundamental part of their twisted ideology to believe in male superiority. The last person anyone would look for is a female."

Crawford nodded in contemplative agreement. "True enough. Their creed is built upon a warped notion of hierarchy, placing men above all else. A woman in charge would be calculated and clever, indeed. However, I believe that introducing a woman into their ranks would be too severe a departure from their established principles. This much we know from Carenza and Nora's run-ins with them."

Rainville, pondering the implication, added, "If we're looking at potential suspects, we might want to remain focused on male members of the *ton* who harbor strong resentment against their peers, especially women. Someone with a grudge and the means to carry out these attacks."

"Let's not rule out the possibility of a splinter faction or a new leader emerging within the Revivalists," Damon replied. "Desperation can lead to drastic changes in ideology and tactics."

"Quiet!" Catamount suddenly whispered, his senses alerting to a change in the shadows ahead and around them. They felt... alive.

A sudden ambush erupted from the murky corners of the narrow alley. Dark, masked figures lunged at Catamount and his brothers, their faces concealed by tattered masks. "Look out!" Catamount shouted, instinctively drawing his concealed dagger and moving with the fluid grace of a seasoned fighter.

The first assailant lunged at him with a rusted blade, but Catamount sidestepped the attack with finesse. He countered with a swift, calculated strike, disarming the assailant with a precise twist of his wrist. The clang of the fallen blade echoed in the confined space.

Crawford, his fists a blur as he fended off another, shouted, "What in bloody hell?" He dodged a swing, countering with a powerful uppercut that sent his opponent reeling. "It's like school fights at Eton all over again."

Rainville grunted. "They must be wanting to relive their glory days."

"Looks like we've got some entertainment, lads." Damon, a bare-knuckle boxer, sidestepped a charging adversary, delivering a precise jab to their midsection. "I do love a good fight."

Catamount, his movements smooth and controlled, dispatched an attacker with a swift strike to his windpipe. "Stay focused! We need answers, not a tavern brawl!"

Crawford, landing a powerful hook, asked, "Why this attack now? It's not Revivalist caliber."

Rainville, with a swift kick to his attacker's gut, replied, "It's not them, period. Too amateurish. This lacks their usual flair and drama."

Damon, grappling with an opponent, agreed, "Someone's pulling the strings, and it's not these unimpressive shites."

"Exactly," the duke replied.

Crawford shouted as he landed a punch on his assailant, "Who sent you? Speak up!"

The attacker, defiant, spat blood at the ground. "You won't stop the Revivalists. Their cause is righteous!"

Rainville groaned and grabbed his assailant's shirt. "Names! We want names, not some deluded rhetoric."

Damon grinned awfully, holding his attacker on his tiptoes

and looking him straight in the eyes. "They always talk. We just need to ask the right questions."

Crawford, fists flying with brutal efficiency, growled, "If they're not Revivalists, who the hell are these bastards?"

Spinning to avoid a knife's edge, Rainville grunted, "Cowards."

Catamount shouted, "These sods don't look like your average street trash!" He dealt with them every day and could spot the difference.

"But they're not peers, either." Crawford fended off a punch. "Look at their hands." He spun and countered with a right cross. "Not soft enough."

An attacker ran at the duke with his knife blade glinting in the dim lantern light. "The Revivalists will rise!"

Rainville, poised and ready, replied, "Enough theatrics. Who's pulling your strings? Who's the leader of the Revivalists?"

Damon joined the duke. "You picked the wrong alley for a scuffle, mate."

With a shout, the attacker launched at them, slicing the air in front of him with his knife. "I will protect the cause!"

Behind him, the other attackers, bruised and bloodied, slipped fast as cats down the alley and away, clearly knowing it was their chance at escape.

"Please," Damon drawled, and pelted the idiot charging them between the eyes with a stone he'd pulled from his pocket.

The attacker dropped to the cobbled street like a... well, stone.

Catamount, a dark smile playing on his lips, leaned down over the subdued attacker. "Congratulations, my friend. You just earned yourself a one-way trip to the holding cell. I've got a lot of questions, and you're going to provide some answers."

The attacker's lips curled into a snarl. "I ain't tellin' you nothin'. You can't stop what's coming. The Revivalists will prevail."

Catamount's grin widened, the shadows casting an ominous

hue on his face. "We'll see about that. I've got ways of making people talk. And this is one conversation that I've waited a long time to have."

CHAPTER NINE

J ULIETTE'S FINGERS TIREDLY worked the last delicate stitches on a gown as evening settled over London. The bell above the door chimed as the last customer left, leaving her alone to tidy up from the busy day.

"Ah, *mon petit chat*, what a day it's been," Juliette murmured to Odette, who had descended from their cozy flat above the modiste shop the moment the door shut. The feline blinked lazily, her fluffy tail curling around her paws.

As Juliette carefully folded fabrics and stored away tools, she recounted the day's events to her attentive companion. "We had Mrs. Marchand in, insisting on a gown for the ball. And then that charming young couple—newly engaged, they said! How delightful. I do adore a good love story."

Odette, seemingly more interested in chasing her own tail, flicked her ears as Juliette continued. "And Captain Castlebury! Did you see him, *mon ami*? That ruggedly handsome man, striding in as if he owned the place. Unusual for such a stern man to grace our shop."

With the last gown neatly stored, Juliette stopped and stretched, her fingers brushing against the kitten's soft fur when she bent down. "There's something about him, *chaton*. Something that tugs at the corners of my thoughts. Those piercing green eyes, so knowing and intense. A mystery, *non?* And he keeps calling me Julie, saying he knows me. Why? I am only

Juliette." She moved to the front of the shop, securing the delicate dresses behind the glass cabinets. "Well, my friend, another day has come to an end. Let's head back upstairs and enjoy a quiet evening together."

The last glimmers of daylight faded outside, casting a muted warmth through the lace curtains of Juliette's shop. The ambiance shifted from the bustling energy of the day to a quieter, more intimate atmosphere. The lingering scent of perfumed customers filled the air as Juliette moved back through the shop, finishing her day's work.

She sighed, a mixture of contentment and restlessness lingering within her. "Ah, my creations, each with a story of its own," she mused, a wistful smile playing on her lips. The shop, with its varied hues and inviting textures, held a timeless charm. A haven where women sought elegance and a touch of the extraordinary in the carefully crafted gowns. She was proud of her place, of what she'd made.

As she moved to the counter, her gaze fell upon a small mirror framed in gilded gold. She caught her own reflection, noting her attire of practicality and fashion. The fabric of her gown flowed gracefully, a muted mulberry tone that complemented her auburn hair and hazel eyes. The dark smudges of worry beneath them were less complementary.

Still, her thoughts continued to stray to Captain Catamount Castlebury. "He's so… commanding, and yet there's a vulnerability," she muttered, her words a quiet confession to the empty shop—and Odette. The conflicting emotions, attraction and doubt, tugged at her. "What is it about him, *mon ami*? Why does his gaze feel like a connection to a past I can't grasp? And that impossible vision of his kiss… What the deuce was that all about?"

Shaking her head at the bizarreness of it, Juliette moved to the door, the brass key cool against her fingertips. She took a lingering glance around the shop, the play of light and shadows casting a subtle spell on her dresses and the mysteries they held.

With a final sigh, she turned the key in the lock, securing the modiste shop for the night.

"Oh," she gasped, recalling that she'd promised to get food for Odette before the end of the day. Caught up in all the busyness of the day, she'd completely forgotten. "I'll get something from the tavern on Cork and be right back."

The soft jingle of the bell above the door marked her departure from the shop as she stepped outside into the cool autumn air. She spun toward the door once more, casting one last glance around to ensure everything was in order. With the shop securely locked, she found herself alone on Bond Street.

Feeling something at her ankles, she glanced down at find Odette rubbing against her. "How did you sneak out so quickly?" Picking her up, she nestled the kitten in her arms and prepared to take her back inside. "I know you're hungry, but you can't go with me to the tavern. I'm sorry, *mon ami.*"

Instead of purring, the kitten hissed and shrank into her arms.

Juliette paused, her intuition sharpening as an uneasy feeling settled upon her. She leaned her back against the shop door, her eyes darting along the low-lit street as she scanned it for anything out of place. "You feel it too, don't you?" she whispered to the kitten, gently stroking Odette's fur.

A faint rustle in the shadows suddenly caught Juliette's attention, and her senses went on high alert. She peered into the darkness, seeking the source of the sound. The sensation of being watched bloomed and quickly intensified.

Juliette stood tall, her gaze flitting nervously between the empty street and the locked door behind her. The kitten nestled closer, Odette's instincts clearly to hide. With a final, lingering look at the quiet street, Juliette whispered reassurances to her feline companion. "It's fine, just a stray animal. Maybe a mouse. Everything is fine, *ma fille.*"

She slid the brass key from her dress pocket and reached behind her for the knob. Fumbling at first, she soon slid it into place and heard the lock unlatch with relief. Together, she and

Odette retreated into the safety of her shop, leaving the mystery of whatever that really was beyond the now-closed door.

The creeping unease lingered, however. Juliette strode through the room, glancing over the mannequins unadorned for the night, the fabric rolls neatly organized on shelves, and the remnants of a day spent attending to customers. Odette, still cradled in her arms, mirrored her apprehension by twitching her whiskers and letting out the occasional hiss. Juliette continued her soft murmurs, trying to soothe them both. But even with the door shut and locked, the sensation of being watched persisted. Like an invisible weight upon her shoulders.

She tightened her grip on the kitten, her footsteps hushed against the polished floorboards. With each passing moment, the feeling of being observed intensified. The gas lamps outside on Bond Street cast elongated shadows that shimmered eerily upon the walls of her shop.

She considered reaching for the comforting weight of the scissors or a pin, as means of self-assurance and protection, but the chilling awareness of an unseen gaze held her frozen to the spot. For several moments she stood there, breathing rapidly. Finally breaking free, she nearly ran toward the staircase leading to her flat above, Odette nestled against her shoulder now, her ears perked and flickering.

The trip upstairs, usually routine and uneventful, seemed to take forever.

At last, she closed the door to her flat behind her and leaned against it, still searching for some intruder, some spy, and thankfully finding none. Odette, sensing her distress, purred softly, offering comfort now that she was home. Despite the reassurance, the disquieting feeling lingered. The scent of lavender sachets permeated the air from Juliette's attempts at creating a tranquil haven amidst the hustle of her daily life.

Her gaze swept across the room as she kicked off her slippers, from the worn but cherished armchair by the window to the small writing desk scattered with sketches and fabric samples.

The teakettle sat on the stove, an invitation to warmth and serenity. "I don't know what's gotten into me tonight," she admitted to the kitten, setting Odette gently on the arm of the chair. "Perhaps it's the talk of the Revivalists with the captain. It's unnerving, isn't it?"

As she busied herself in the compact kitchen, the rhythmic sounds of water pouring into a teapot provided a comforting backdrop to her murmured thoughts. The aroma of chamomile and lavender filled the air as she prepared the soothing brew, a ritual designed to dissipate any lingering disquiet. "The city has a way of seeping into your bones," she continued, the words more for her own reassurance than for the attentive kitten's. "These streets hold echoes, stories. Tonight feels different, though. As if they are whispering secrets about *me*. Watching *me*. I don't like it."

Juliette strained the tea and cradled the warm teacup in her hands. The fragrant steam rose in delicate tendrils. She settled into the armchair, the plush cushions embracing her as she gazed out of the window, seeking peace in the quiet of her flat. Her safe place. Odette was her furry, silent companion as they listened to the muted city sounds. She sipped her tea, the calming blend weaving a spell of tranquility around her, even as the vague unease persisted in the recesses of her mind.

As Juliette sat in the quiet, the lingering unease took on a more palpable form, like a ghostly whisper brushing against the recesses of her consciousness. The soft hum of the city outside seemed to fade as a flicker of something dark and painful danced at the edge of her awareness—a memory?

A tremor of discomfort coursed through her, and she instinctively recoiled from the encroaching tendrils of the elusive memory, a vision she instinctively did not want to see. The teacup tipped precariously in her hand. She jerked and shifted her gaze, choosing to focus on the sketches and fabric samples scattered across her writing desk—a deliberate distraction from the haunting unknown that pushed at the edges of her consciousness. Sweat broke out along her brow. Her breath shortened.

"It's nothing," she murmured to herself. "Just a trick of my mind, perhaps. All the Revivalist talk has unsettled me, that's all."

The kitten, ever attuned to her moods, nestled closer, offering a comforting presence. Juliette absent-mindedly traced the patterns on the teacup, as if seeking grounding in the tactile sensation.

A sudden crash echoed through her flat, shattering the tranquility that had just resettled over it. Her heart pounded as she recognized the sound of breaking glass. "No!" Leaping to her feet, she rushed to the nearest window, dread clawing at her chest, and her eyes widened at the sight of a fading figure disappearing down Bond Street toward Savile Row, and out of sight. Bricks, thrown with malicious intent, littered the sidewalk in front of her modiste shop. Shattered glass from her front window lay with them.

Juliette gasped. The window, a barrier between her sanctuary and the outside world, had been breached and violated. The shards of glass glittered like malevolent confetti on the street below, and Juliette's hands trembled as she pressed them against the cool surface of the second-floor window frame. "Why?" she whispered.

Tears threatened as she surveyed the aftermath of the vandalized shop below. She was shaken. Truly shaken.

It was time to seek the help offered from Captain Castlebury.

"*Mon Dieu*," she uttered, her voice a shaky whisper as she looked at the mess below. "This is madness. What could anyone want with me?"

Odette, already curled back up in the chair, blinked at her.

Closing her eyes briefly, Juliette drew in a steadying breath. She had been hesitant, grappling with uncertainties about the startling connection between her and the captain. Yet this... *intrusion*, this violation of the space she had worked so hard to build, pushed her past the threshold of reluctance.

"Captain Castlebury," she murmured, pacing the room with an anxious energy. "I never thought I'd seek his help again, but this… this is beyond what I can handle alone." She glanced at the kitten, seeking some form of reassurance in her innocent gaze. "*Oui*, I'm going to do it."

Juliette descended the stairs from her flat to the downstairs shop. Across the room, the shattered window gaped like a wound. Gathering what remained of her composure, she made her way to the door, stepping over the bricks that littered the floor, intent on seeking assistance from the one person who had unwittingly become a central figure in the unraveling mysteries of her life.

The gas lamps cast a feeble glow as she stepped into the cool night air. "Let's try this again. To the Bow Street Runners' headquarters and Captain Castlebury I go."

Shards of the front window lay scattered like broken dreams around her.

Fear clutched at her as she surveyed the damage, her unsteady hands reaching for the door to pull it shut. Among the wreckage at her feet, a glimmer caught her eye—a note, tied to one of the bricks. Trepidation seized her as she hesitated for a moment, dread intensifying. Nevertheless, her determination pushed her forward, and she gingerly picked up the brick with the note, reading: *We know who you are.*

The taunting, terrifying words leapt off the paper, freezing her blood. With a deep breath, Juliette clutched the note tightly, scanning the street, more than half expecting the unseen adversary to materialize.

The offer of help from Captain Castlebury suddenly seemed like a lifeline.

CHAPTER TEN

THE DAMP, BARELY lit holding cells of the Bow Street Runners' headquarters exuded an air of foreboding as Catamount descended into their depths. The echoes of muffled sounds and distant footsteps reverberated off the cold stone walls. Behind the thick iron bars, a lone figure slouched against the damp stones, shackled and battered from Damon's solid arse kicking.

Catamount approached with the confidence of a veteran detective, taking everything in and assessing, memorizing. The clinking of keys resonated in the corridor as the turnkey unlocked the cell, granting him access to the captive inside.

"What's your name?" Catamount demanded when he stepped in, his voice sharp and authoritative.

The captive, a disheveled man with a bruised face, shot a defiant glare at him. "Don't matter none. I ain't tellin' you nothin'. Not my name or nothin'."

Catamount leaned in toward him. "You attacked my men in St. Giles. You'll talk, whether you want to or not." His fingers brushed against the battered edge of a file he held detailing the man's assault. "You don't want a one-way trip to Newgate, do you? Because I can make that happen."

The man's bravado wavered, and he spat out a stream of curses. "You weaselcock! You can't prove nothin'."

"Maybe not yet. But I can make your stay in the cells a living hell until we get what we need. And I can charge you with assaulting an officer. *Me.*"

"But I didn't clock you! That weren't me!"

As the interrogation unfolded, Catamount employed a mix of intimidation and persuasion tactics. He pried information from the man, piece by piece, leveraging his expertise as a relentless detective. Their conversation reverberated through the cold, unforgiving cells as it grew heated.

Catamount's sleeves were rolled up, revealing the sinewy strength in his arms as he leaned against the bars. The scent of dampness and desperation clung to the air as the gritty reality of detective work unfolded in the bowels of the Runners' headquarters. He was unyielding in his quest for answers.

"You're covering for them, aren't you? What's your connection to the Revivalists?"

The man spat on the ground. "I don't know what you're talkin' about. They don't deal with folks like me. They're purebloods, they are. I ain't one of 'em. Me and my gang—we admire them, that's all."

Catamount leaned back, the cold metal bars pressing against his shoulders. "Purebloods or not, they attack innocent people. I aim to bring them to justice, and you're going to help me."

A sly grin twisted the man's lips. "You can't touch 'em. They're above the law. You're wastin' your time."

With a sudden, swift motion, Catamount launched forward and grabbed the collar of the man's shirt, his face inches away. "I don't care if they think they're above the law. Nobody is. You're going to tell me everything you know about the Revivalists, or you'll find out just how creative I can get in making your stay here unbearable. I have very little patience for people like you." Then, maintaining his firm grip on the man's collar, he leaned in even further. "Give me names. Since you love and admire them so much. Who's running the Revivalists? Tell me the nobles behind this, and maybe, just maybe, I'll put in a word to lighten your sentence. It's the only chance you've got."

The man hesitated, glancing around the dingy cell as if considering the offer. Finally, with a resigned sigh, he muttered, "Lord Harrington and his wife, Lady Eleanor. They're the ones pulling the strings."

Catamount committed the names to memory. "Good. Now, you better be truthful about this. I'll be watching, and if you've fed me lies, your fate won't be any better than the last man who lied to me."

"What happened to him?"

"He's dead." Catamount's eyes narrowed suddenly with thought. "So it's a woman behind the Revivalists all along. I did not expect that."

The man's lips curled into a sly smile, and he met Catamount's gaze with a defiant glint in his eyes, his laughter taunting. "Sorry, captain, but you've got it all wrong. The Revivalists, they're a noble bunch, purebloods through and through. No women involved. Just a club for gentlemen with a taste for the thrill of the forbidden."

Catamount realized the man was feeding him a pack of lies. "You just named Lady Eleanor!" he growled, his temper flaring. Frustration boiled within him. "You're playing games, and I'm running out of patience. Tell me right now who's pulling the strings behind the Revivalists, or you'll find out just how much I can push before you break."

The man's smirk wavered for a split second, a flicker of uncertainty crossing his face. Yet he remained defiant, a challenge gleaming in his eyes.

"Just tell us who's leading the Revivalists, and maybe we can cut a deal," Catamount growled, his patience wearing thin.

The thug chuckled, a mirthless sound that grated on Catamount's nerves. "You think I'd betray my heroes for a deal with the likes of you?"

Ready to storm out in exasperation, Catamount froze when the man's tone shifted, a dark edge creeping into his words.

"Ah, Captain Castlebury, the great Bow Street Runner. A man haunted by the ghosts of the past. Or should I say, haunted by a certain *woman?*"

Catamount's knuckles whitened as the mention of Julie sliced through the air like a blade. He fixed the man with a steely gaze. "You don't know anything about her," Catamount spat, his voice low and dangerous.

The man leaned back. "Oh, I know more than you think. Maybe you should ask yourself why she's still haunting you. Or better yet, why you couldn't protect her that night."

Catamount's breath caught, the wounds of the past suddenly raw and exposed once more. He stood there, unexpectedly grappling with the weight of his loss.

The holding cell seemed to close in around him, the echoes of Julie's absence resounding in the stark silence. Catamount's fists clenched, the desire for violence bubbling beneath his surface. A surge of fury coursed through him, but he fought to maintain control.

"You seem mighty interested in that French dressmaker lady these days," the man taunted him, a cruel gleam in his eyes. "Captain Catamount Castlebury, sniffing around where he shouldn't."

His gaze locked on the smirking thug. The desire to lash out, to wipe that mocking grin off the man's face, clawed at him. Yet he knew the importance of keeping a semblance of composure. He took a deep breath, the controlled façade of the experienced detective settling back into place. "I'm here for justice, not your baseless provocations," Catamount retorted. "You spread the word. Tell the Revivalists that Catamount Castlebury is coming for them. They can't escape me."

The man's eyes widened, and he swallowed—hard. A bead of sweat trickled down his temple.

Catamount's gaze sharpened as a sudden realization hit him. "Bloody hell!" he cursed.

In an instant, the man's face contorted, and he began foaming at the mouth.

Catamount's grip tightened on the thug's collar as he yelled,

"I won't let them win! You hear me?" The words echoed through the grimy confines of the holding cell, a defiant declaration against the poisonous gambit the man had chosen.

Desperation and frustration surged within Catamount as the man convulsed in his grasp. The poison pill had stolen his chance to uncover the Revivalists. His only lead gone.

Back to square one.

He released the lifeless form, then straightened up, taking a deep breath to compose himself. The cell felt suffocating, and the weight of the unanswered questions pressed down on him. He turned on his heel, leaving the holding cell behind, his mind already calculating the next move in the dangerous game the Revivalists were hellbent on continuing.

As he stepped out into the corridors, his jaw began to twitch. The hunt for the Revivalists had taken an unexpected turn, but it hadn't dimmed the fire within him. If anything, it fueled the determination to dismantle the nefarious group that had haunted him for far too long.

Juliette.

Bollocks, he'd nearly forgotten.

They'd been watching him with Juliette.

"Damn," he spat, striding through the lobby.

He left the building, driven by a relentless urgency. The evening shadows clung to the cobblestone streets and his senses were on high alert as he arrived at Juliette's modiste shop. He wasted no time, the sense of urgency propelling his steps toward the door, leaving him blinded to all else around him. His fist hammered on the wood, each rap echoing through the quiet street. Breathless, he awaited her response.

The door to her shop swung open, revealing Juliette, her expression a mixture of surprise and concern. Her modiste's apron hinted at the day's work, but her eyes held a glimmer of relief. "Captain Castlebury? Thank goodness you're here!" she exclaimed. "I was just on my way to Bow Street."

Catamount, his chest rising and falling with the intensity of his feelings, met her gaze. "They know you're connected to me," he stated. "The Revivalists. They know."

Fear flickered in Juliette's beautiful hazel eyes, mirroring the concern surely etched on his face. The threat had become palpable, a sinister presence looming over the modiste shop. As they stood in the doorway, the air crackled around them with unspoken tension.

Catamount's resolve solidified. "I won't let them harm you," he vowed. "I'm moving in," he suddenly declared, his tone flat and eyes deadly serious.

"Captain, you can't just—" she began, but he cut her off with a stern look.

"I can and I will," he asserted. "They know about you and me. I won't let them use you against me. It's not negotiable. Besides, I see the broken window next to me. You're getting a roommate."

The quiet resolve in his voice brooked no argument.

CHAPTER ELEVEN

J ULIETTE FROZE AS Castlebury pushed his way into her closed modiste shop with a determination that shocked her. The contrast between the rugged, imposing figure of the Bow Street Runner and the feminine space of her shop was stark. The scent of fabric and delicate perfumes mingled with the undeniable aura of a man used to navigating the grittier corners of London.

He smelled like wet cobblestones and parchment.

It was… appealing.

"Captain, you can't just barge in like this!" she protested again, surprised and flustered. She watched as he surveyed the surroundings, his eyes sharp and vigilant.

"I can and I will," he repeated, his tone unyielding. "I won't let them catch you unguarded. These Revivalists mean business, and I'm not taking any chances."

Her protest died on her lips as he moved with a certain familiarity through the space. The dainty fabrics and elegant gowns seemed to shrink in comparison to the masculine presence that now filled the room. Juliette found herself torn between irritation and a strange sense of reassurance.

"What about my business? My customers?" she demanded, though the words came out more as an exclamation of disbelief than a coherent question.

"They'll have to manage with me here," he replied, not bothering to soften the blow. "This is about keeping you safe,

Juliette."

Her name spoken in that authoritative tone sent a shiver down her spine. The reality of his intrusion settled in, and she felt frustration but also a strange gratitude. The shadows of the recent threats lingered, and having him in her shop felt like a shield against the encroaching darkness.

As he moved further into the space, a sense of vulnerability swept over Juliette. "You don't get to decide everything, captain," she said, trying to assert some semblance of control. "This is my shop, my life." Not that she hadn't realized earlier how much she needed his help. It was just that it mattered, having a say in things.

Catamount turned to face her. "And I won't stand by while they threaten it. Whether you like it or not, we're in this together now."

"Well, captain, if you're going to invade my space, at least do it with some finesse. You can't just barge in and declare martial law," she challenged.

He raised an eyebrow, a wry smirk playing on his lips. "Finesse is not exactly my specialty, *mademoiselle*. I prefer the direct approach."

She rolled her eyes, unable to suppress a smile. "Direct, invasive—it's all the same to you, isn't it?"

Castlebury chuckled, a low, rumbling sound that reverberated through the small shop. "When it comes to keeping you safe, yes. I don't have the luxury of finesse."

Juliette crossed her arms. "And what makes you think I need saving? I've managed just fine without a hulking Bow Street Runner barging into my life."

"The broken window and shattered glass tells me you need saving." His eyes locked on to hers, his gaze intense. "These Revivalists are not to be trifled with. You're not safe from their reach."

We know who you are.

A flicker of vulnerability flashed through Juliette before she masked it with a defiant tilt of her chin. "I can handle myself, captain. I don't need a protector."

Oh, but she did. She knew she did. Her broken window was proof.

Catamount stepped closer, his shoulders impossibly broad. "Humor me, Juliette. I've seen too much darkness to stand by idly when I can do something about it."

She sighed with resignation. "Fine. But you can't just move in without any ground rules. This is still my shop, my home."

He inclined his head, a smile playing on his firm, serious lips. "Agreed. As long as you understand that I'm not here to play tea parties. We're dealing with dangerous individuals."

"Oh, I'm well aware."

Catamount surveyed her shop. "Walk me through what happened here," he demanded, his tone no-nonsense.

Juliette hesitated for a moment before admitting, "I was upstairs when it happened. Bricks came crashing through the shop window, and there was a note."

"Show me the brick with the note."

Leading him to the damaged window, Juliette pointed to the brick on the floor. Catamount picked it up, examining it with a furrowed brow.

"Did you touch this?" he asked sharply.

"No… Well, yes. But I left it exactly where it fell," Juliette replied, her eyes tracking his every move. "I only picked it up to read what it said and then I returned it to where it landed."

Catamount turned his attention to the note. She watched on as he scanned the taunting words, and his expression darkened. "They're watching you closely," he muttered, pacing back and forth. "We need to take this seriously, Juliette. These threats are not to be ignored. I won't let anything happen to you."

"Captain—"

"Catamount." He raked a long-fingered hand through his hair, looking almost frazzled. "Devil's bollocks, just call me Catamount. Or Cat. Just nothing so formal, since I'm moving in with you."

"I can handle myself, *captain*. I don't need a watchdog. A helping hand, certainly. But not a guard."

He shot her a stern look. "*Catamount*. This is not a game. We're dealing with dangerous individuals. I need you to follow my lead on this."

Fine. She could drop the formality for now.

Catamount's piercing gaze softened as he looked into her eyes. His voice, usually gruff and commanding, turned low, warm, and intimately close. "I won't lose you again, Juliette," he murmured, a promise hanging in the air between them.

Juliette's heart fluttered in response to the sincerity in his eyes. There was a vulnerability in Catamount's expression that transcended the stoic exterior he often wore. For a moment, the world outside their bubble seemed to fade away. In that quiet assurance, Juliette sensed a connection that surpassed the immediate threats surrounding them. Catamount's declaration echoed with a depth that resonated within her, touching a place she hadn't realized existed.

The modiste shop, usually bustling with creativity, now became a backdrop for a more personal revelation. Catamount's impending move-in, initially met with resistance, took on a new dimension. It wasn't just about protection; it was a declaration, an acknowledgment of something unspoken.

As if compelled by an irresistible force, Catamount enveloped her in his strong arms. The weight of his protective embrace felt like a shield against the looming threats outside. Their lips met in a tender kiss, and she found herself yielding to the intensity of the connection between them.

The kiss lingered, a fusion of longing, assurance, and the uncharted territories of their intertwined destinies. In that stolen moment, the troubles that shadowed them seemed to recede, replaced by the warmth of shared emotion. The chemistry between them crackled.

Juliette, caught in the heat of the moment, flung her arms

around his neck and kissed him back with every ounce of feeling for him she didn't realize she had.

He held her in a protective embrace, the warmth of his presence both comforting and electrifying. In that intimate closeness, his green eyes bored into hers, searching. "You taste the same," Catamount said in a low, warm murmur, his breath mingling with hers in the charged air. The words hung between them, carrying the weight of shared memories she couldn't recall.

As he murmured, "Julie," against her lips, a shiver ran down Juliette's spine. The familiarity in his voice stirred something deep within her—a resonance that echoed through the recesses of forgotten moments. Time itself seemed to hold its breath as the past and present converged in that tender, stolen moment.

Catamount's lips took hers with a depth of feeling that transcended words. The air crackled with a potent blend of intimacy and longing. As he kissed her again, the connection deepened, a magnetic pull that stirred echoes of familiarity within her. The depth of the kiss sparked jolts of recognition, zinging through her like an electrifying current. She felt it—the inexplicable familiarity in the way his lips moved against hers, the sense of his touch.

Exactly like her impossible vision from earlier.

Keeping those jolts of recognition to herself, Juliette surrendered to the moment, allowing the kiss to weave a tapestry of emotion that defied the gaps in her memory. Wrapped in the arms of a man who felt both known and unknown, she fell into the undeniable pull of the present.

With a reluctant expression, Catamount pulled back, his eyes holding a resolute gleam. "I'll send for one of my men to collect my things," he stated.

Juliette sighed inwardly and chided herself for finding his determination attractive. As the reality of Catamount moving in settled in, she nearly laughed. Two weeks ago, she would never have guessed this was where she would be.

Strange how life changed.

As she led Catamount upstairs to her modest living quarters, she was acutely aware of the intimacy of her small, private space. As they entered her bedchamber, she hesitated for a moment. "I'm afraid there's only one bed. You'll have to make do on the floor for the time being," she said.

He nodded. "Not an issue. I've slept in worse places."

A complicated blend of relief and disquiet rushed through her. She wanted to maintain a professional distance, yet the reality of sharing such an intimate space with him stirred conflicting emotions within her. The air in the room seemed charged with *so* many possibilities. "There are blankets in the armoire," she said, her voice unsteady as she sought to redirect her focus to practical matters.

"Appreciate it," Catamount replied, his eyes meeting hers with a directness that sent a shiver down her spine.

As Juliette left him to settle in, her thoughts swirled with curiosity. What did he think of her modest bedchamber? Did he notice the subtle fragrance of lavender in the air—just a touch that lingered from her favorite candle? Her gaze flitted to the small shelf filled with cherished books and trinkets, and she wondered if he took note of the personal touches that spoke of her life beyond the modiste shop. If so, what did he think of them?

What were his impressions—of the delicate lace curtains that allowed a gentle stream of moonlight into the room, of the worn rug beneath his feet, of the very bed where she slept alone?

As she busied herself in the small kitchen, preparing tea and organizing her thoughts, Juliette couldn't shake the awareness that, beneath the surface of their chatter and shared purpose, there was a delicate dance unfolding—one that held the potential to reveal desires that lingered in the quiet spaces between their breaths. That kiss had destroyed everything she thought she'd known about kissing. About *feeling*.

As she returned with a tray carrying two steaming cups of tea, she found Catamount in the middle of settling down for the night. A gasp caught in her throat as her eyes traced the contours of his shirtless form. His well-defined muscles played beneath the surface, sculpted by a life lived outside the ballrooms of Mayfair. The flickering lamplight cast intriguing shadows across his broad shoulders and the rugged terrain of his back as he made a bed from blankets he had retrieved from her nearby armoire. Juliette struggled to maintain composure as she drank in the sight of him, her grip on the tray faltering for an instant as she tried without success to avert her gaze.

Catamount, sensing her presence, looked up from his bed with a hint of amusement in his liquid green eyes. "Tea, mademoiselle? Or are you just here to admire the view?"

Juliette's cheeks flushed, and she attempted a smile. "Tea, of course. You can keep your ego leashed."

He chuckled, the rare sound sending a warm current through her belly. "Ego? I am just a humble Bow Street Runner trying to get some sleep."

As she handed him a cup of her finest chamomile and lavender blend, their fingers brushed briefly, and Juliette couldn't deny the jolt of awareness that passed between them.

Catamount, with an uncharacteristic grin, took a sip and sat at her tiny table next to the fireplace, his gaze lingering on her face. "What's on your mind, Juliette? You seem a bit flustered."

She bit her lower lip, feigning nonchalance, though in truth she was rather flustered. She had a half-naked man in her bedchamber! Any sensible woman would be flummoxed. "Nothing, captain, er, Catamount. Just... surprised to find a shirtless detective in my home." And it felt oddly new and *not* new at the same time. It somehow felt... *right*.

Catamount's eyes suddenly heated with something that looked a lot like affection as he gazed at her. Perhaps even love. He didn't love her, though, so it couldn't be that. But it was *something*.

And she didn't object to it.

He glanced down at his flat, chiseled stomach, and grinned. "A hazard of the job, unfortunately. Terrible stain of unknown origin on that tunic I was wearing that smelled vaguely of vomit from a vagrant I arrested earlier. I couldn't stand the smell of it near my nostrils for another moment—and certainly not overnight. Honestly, I have changes of clothes stashed around half of London. My flat, my brother's place in Belgravia, the family shipping company's office at the docks. As well as my office at Bow Street. Because Runner work is entirely lacking in glamour, and I often end up smelling of something unpleasant. Now, shall we enjoy our tea, or do you want me to come up with more surprises?"

Juliette put down the tray and sat across from him, attempting to regain her composure. "Tea it is. No more surprises for tonight, thank you."

As he leaned back in his chair, his gaze locked on to hers with a sudden intensity that sent shivers down her spine. The playful flirtation lingered in the air like a thin veil, masking the underlying currents of something deeper, something that had started to unfurl between them. How was she supposed to even begin focusing on what that might be, however, when he just sat there across from her, bare chested and glorious, like it was the most natural thing in the world?

Catamount's voice, low and velvety, broke the brief silence. "You know, this might be the quietest room in all of London. A bit too quiet, don't you think? Why don't you tell me about yourself? I want to get to know the woman who managed to turn my world upside down with a single look."

The atmosphere between them crackled with strange tension, and Juliette nearly shook with excitement and trepidation. The small table they sat at seemed to shrink even further, closing the distance between them. "I-I don't know what you mean," she stammered.

Catamount set his tea aside, his gaze never leaving hers. "Tell me, what's beneath the surface? What secrets are you hiding behind those extraordinary hazel eyes?"

She hesitated for a moment, pricked by a rush of vulnerability. "We all have our secrets. Some are just better at hiding them than others."

He leaned forward. "I'm not one to shy away from a challenge. When there's a mystery, I'm determined to unravel it. It's what I do."

Juliette, caught in the magnetic pull of his gaze, felt a surge of conflicting emotions. "I assure you, there are no secrets to unravel here," she replied, attempting to sound confident, though uncertainty lingered in her eyes and heart.

Catamount leaned back, a thoughtful expression crossing his rugged features, and he scratched lazily at an itch on his lower belly, drawing her attention. But she refused to look. It was too dangerous. Too… enticing.

"Everyone has something to hide, Juliette," he said. "It's always only a matter of time before the truth comes to light."

The mention of truth sent a shiver down her spine. Unbidden images flickered in her mind—flashes of a terrifying, fuzzy past intertwined with the terrible presence of the Revivalists. Juliette felt a knot tighten in her stomach, a sense of foreboding that she couldn't shake. Her palms went sweaty.

"I've seen my fair share of mysteries in the dark corners of this city," Catamount continued. "If there's something you're not telling me, it's better to bring it to light now."

She hesitated, caught between the desire for transparency and the fear of what those buried memories might reveal. "I… I don't know what you're talking about. I'm just a modiste trying to make a living. No mysteries here." Other than the one about why she couldn't remember her own life. Small thing, that.

He nodded, as if he'd expected resistance. "Very well. But remember, when the truth catches up, it's best to face it head-on. I'm here to help, whether you believe it or not." He stood, his body powerful and sleek and mesmerizing.

The room fell into a hushed stillness as Catamount settled onto his makeshift bedding, and she stripped to her shift behind a screen and then settled onto hers. The dim glow of a lone lantern cast shifting shadows along the wall, heightening the tension that already seemed to crackle in the air. As his gaze met hers, a softness crept into his eyes—a vulnerability that seemed at odds with the hardened detective she had come to know recently. He whispered, "Goodnight, Julie."

The simple endearment, spoken in the privacy of her home, carried a familiarity that tugged at the edges of her consciousness. Her heart squeezed in response. "Goodnight," she replied, her voice a breathy murmur.

The cadence of Catamount's steady breathing created a lulling rhythm in the quiet confines of her flat. As she surrendered to the embrace of her own slumber, two realizations crystallized in the recesses of her mind.

First, she hadn't corrected him when he used the wrong name. The slip lingered like a silent agreement, a tacit acknowledgment that in that moment "Julie" had felt right. It was a subtle thread connecting them on a more personal level. One she no longer fought against.

Second, Catamount's presence beside her, the simplicity of shared breaths and soft sounds of sleep, resonated in her chest with a peculiar sense of longing. The night, usually solitary and silent, held a different texture—a warmth she had unknowingly craved. The intimacy of their proximity cocooned them in the darkness.

As Juliette drifted into the realms of dreams, the mysteries of her past and Catamount became threads woven into the fabric of her consciousness, awaiting unraveling with the dawn of a new day.

CHAPTER TWELVE

LATER THAT NIGHT, her usual sanctuary of sleep morphed into a battleground, where nightmares waged war on her. She thrashed beneath her sheets, ensnared in the clutches of unseen tormentors. Men with masks and horrible, oily laughs. Cold sweat and fear clung to her skin as the dreams unfurled, painting a grotesque image of menace and malevolence.

In the hushed hours of the night, Juliette's restless murmurs intensified. Words spilled forth, half formed and fragmented, echoing the terror that gripped her in the dream realm. "Please, no… Don't…" The words tumbled from her lips, desperate pleas entwined with the horrible laughter of nightmares that haunted her. She smelled the acrid scent of smoke, fire vivid in the recesses of her nightmares, swallowing wood and walls and anyone left inside. "Stop! Someone, help!"

Suddenly the torment dissolved as a deep, soothing voice cut through the terror, wrapping around Juliette like a protective blanket. The harsh edges of her nightmares softened as warmth and strength enveloped her. In the dimness of her room, she felt him pull her close, protecting her. Catamount anchored her, his sturdy arms pulling her from the clutches of her subconscious demons.

"Easy now, Julie. You're safe," he murmured. His hand, firm and gentle, traced comforting circles on her back as she nestled against his bare chest. The rhythmic rise and fall of his breath became a calming lullaby, a stark contrast to the disarray of her dreams.

Juliette's nightgown clung to her, bunched around her thighs. She tucked into him and let him hold her.

"You're safe with me," he continued. "I won't let anything harm you. I've got you."

Juliette nuzzled into the crook of his neck, seeking refuge in the solid warmth he provided. His heart beat beneath her touch, a steady rhythm that synchronized with her own. The scent of him—musky and somehow familiar—wrapped around her.

As she clung to him, the remnants of the nightmare began to dissipate. The terrible visions, once vivid and tormenting, receded like shadows chased away by the dawn.

He said again, "You're safe. Nothing can harm you now," like he knew how much she needed to hear that over and over like a mantra.

Juliette felt the resonance of his voice deep within her. The intimacy of the moment wove a connection that defied explanation. He'd called her his Julie, a name that reverberated around her heart with a resonance that went beyond the confines of their current reality. Catamount seemed to belong where the present and past that she could remember converged.

As if drawn by an invisible force, their lips met in a luxurious, lingering kiss. The world outside seemed to fade away, leaving only the heat of the connection they forged in the quiet hours of the night. The taste of shared history lingered between them. In that stolen moment, the kiss, a symphony of emotion and unspoken truths, became a bridge between memories and the tangible present.

As they finally parted, breaths mingling in the shared space, the air seemed charged with promise. They lay entangled on her bed in the aftermath of their kiss. Simply feeling each other. Simply *being*.

She drifted to sleep in his arms.

Later, with the soft light of dawn filtering through the curtains, Catamount gently extricated himself from their embrace, leaving a lingering warmth in the space between them. With a half-smile, he leaned down to press a tender kiss on her forehead as she stared groggily up at him. "How about some breakfast?" he suggested. "I can whip up something decent."

Juliette, still caught in the hazy aftermath of the night's shared moments, blinked in mild disbelief. "You can cook?"

He grinned, a playful glint in his eyes. "Well, every Bow Street Runner has a few hidden talents. Cooking happens to be one of mine."

As he headed toward her tiny kitchen, Juliette marveled from her nest at the incongruity of the situation. "I never would've guessed. What's your specialty, then? Arresting criminals or making a delectable omelet?"

Catamount chuckled, the raspy sound echoing in the small space. "Why not do both? But this morning, let's go with omelets. What do you say?"

She nodded, a bemused smile playing on her lips. "Omelets it is, then. But no arresting criminals in my kitchen, please."

Too curious to resist, Juliette climbed from her bed and put on a dressing gown before following him. She leaned against the kitchen counter as she observed Catamount in the midst of domesticity. The morning sunlight kissed his tanned skin, accentuating the rugged contours of his face. His movements were fluid, a mix of grace and raw masculinity that held her captivated. There was a certain allure in witnessing this side of him—the Bow Street Runner with a penchant for cooking. As he cracked eggs into a bowl and whisked them with practiced ease, a cascade of thoughts and emotions surged within her.

The contrast between the hardened detective and the man navigating her kitchen stirred something deep within her. His presence exuded strength and protection, yet the way he handled the ingredients hinted at a gentleness that hid beyond the surface. She couldn't deny the pull of his rugged charm.

Lost in her thoughts, Juliette watched on, appreciating the

way his shirt (a clean one—how had he managed that so fast?) clung to the contours of his muscles as he moved. Curiosity, attraction, and a tinge of vulnerability she hadn't expected swept through her.

A swirl of emotions and questions mingled within her. The sizzling sounds and enticing aromas filled the space, creating a tableau of domesticity that seemed both surreal and comforting. She couldn't shake the feeling of being caught in the crossroads of two worlds—his world of investigations, danger, and the relentless pursuit of justice, and her world of delicate fabrics, fashion, and the pursuit of beauty. The man who had barged into her life now stood before her, effortlessly flipping omelets in a pan.

Juliette's eyes lingered on his strong hands. Questions surfaced in her mind, swirling like the fragrant steam rising from the skillet. What did his presence mean for her peaceful modiste shop? How did he seamlessly transition from the stern detective interrogating criminals to the man flipping omelets in her kitchen?

He turned to face her with a charming smile as the scent of breakfast hung in the air. Juliette's nerves prickled, a sudden wave of disquiet sweeping over her. The cozy familiarity of the kitchen, the shared laughter, and the easy banter clawed at the corner of her mind where elusive memories hid.

In a sudden surge of anxiety, she shoved from the counter and excused herself, feigning a need to check on her shop below. She rushed into her bedchamber and changed briskly, almost frantically, fumbling with the buttons of her dress. She suddenly couldn't stay here, in this domestic space with him.

"Everything all right?" Catamount's voice carried concern as she swept back through, but she couldn't bear to look him in the eyes. Her gaze darted around the room, searching for an escape route. She needed space, air, anything to shake off the disquiet that clung to her. She wasn't sure what was happening, only that she felt agitated in a way she'd never before experienced.

"I just remembered an appointment I'd forgotten," she lied, smoothing down her blue dress with hurried motions. "I need to tend to some customers. Business calls—you know how it is."

His expression shifted, a flicker of disappointment. "Of course. Duty calls."

She forced a smile, avoiding the intensity of his gaze. "Thank you for breakfast, but I'll have to pass. I'll be back later."

As she made her hasty exit from her flat, the stairwell landing was a welcome reprieve. Each step away from the cozy kitchen brought a measure of relief, yet the nagging questions and the elusive memories lingered like cobwebs in the corners of her mind.

Outside the shop, the streets of Mayfair stretched before Juliette as she navigated the bustling thoroughfares, thoughts weaving erratically through her mind. The need for a confidante, someone to unravel the tangled threads of her mind, pushed her on. A friend who could help her decipher the strange visions and keep her secrets. But who?

As she wandered down the sidewalk and deeper into the recesses of her own memories—or the lack thereof—a peculiar revelation dawned. *Julie* wasn't alone—she had Catamount. The profound warmth that accompanied that acknowledgment stirred something deep within her. It wasn't just the passionate kisses or the intimate moments. He cared. Really, truly cared about her. She'd seen that glimpse in his eye. *Julie* had been loved.

By Catamount.

As the streets unfurled with each step she took, she contemplated the mystery that was Catamount Castlebury. A man who seemed to know more about her than she did herself. A man whose presence invoked a sense of security, a flicker of recognition that eluded the rest of her fragmented memories. The yearning for answers pulsed beneath her skin, the desire to understand the intricate dance between herself, *Julie*, and Catamount. She yearned for connection.

The truth hit Juliette like a sudden downpour, drenching her with understanding. She walked the crowded streets, and a veil lifted, revealing the stark truth. The absence of friends, the longing for confidantes—those were her life. The life of Juliette Toussaint, the modiste.

A pang of something deep and resonant surged through her. She wanted to be Julie, to have that connection with someone. It wasn't just about memories or forgotten laughter. It was about the person—the person who had Catamount Castlebury. The person she wished she could be.

The yearning became a palpable force, urging her to understand the complex connection between Julie and the man who seemed to hold the key to her forgotten self. A gasp escaped her lips. Catamount Castlebury wasn't just a fragment of *Julie's* past; he was the very essence of her existence.

She thought of that look in his eye again. *Love.* She wanted that. Fiercely and with all her being.

But what if she wasn't this Julie he seemed to think she was? What if she was just Juliette Toussaint, the Frenchwoman with the faulty memory? Would he look at *her* with love?

Perhaps this connection she felt only existed because she looked like his Julie. Gah, it was tricky, and it seemed like she only knew portions, paragraphs of a bigger piece.

Catamount Castlebury wasn't just a chapter; he was a whole complicated story.

CHAPTER THIRTEEN

CATAMOUNT SAT BEHIND the cluttered desk in his office at Bow Street headquarters, surrounded by stacks of case reports and the low hum of activity filtering in from the bustling streets of London below. His piercing green eyes, usually sharp and focused, carried a distant glint, betraying a mind preoccupied with thoughts that extended far beyond the ink-stained papers strewn across his desk. The scent of aged leather and musty parchment permeated the room, blending with the muted sounds of footsteps echoing through the narrow corridors.

"Focus, Castlebury," he muttered to himself. "You've got a job to do, and it doesn't involve daydreaming about a certain modiste." He picked up a case report, scanning the words, but the letters blurred into an indistinct jumble. The image of Juliette's auburn hair and hazel eyes lingered in his mind, distracting him from the task at hand. With a shake of his head, he attempted to brush off the intrusive thoughts.

The creak of the office door interrupted his internal struggle. Detective Bradley, a seasoned officer with salt-and-pepper hair, entered the room. "Captain, we've got updates on the Revivalist investigation. Some promising leads in the Docklands from that journal of Lord Arnold's."

Catamount nodded, grateful for the shift in focus. "Good. Bring me the details. Let's see if we can finally put an end to this madness."

As Bradley left to retrieve the information, Catamount rubbed his temples, trying to dispel the lingering image of Juliette's face. The complexities of his personal life clashed with the gritty realities of his profession. Juliette was beautiful. His job was most often ugly.

"Here's the file," Bradley said as he reentered the room and handed it over.

As Catamount perused the new leads, his thoughts stubbornly circled back to Juliette. The events of the past days had stirred a dormant ache, one that whispered of a connection he was unwilling to dismiss. His mind replayed moments—her startled gaze, the familiar flutter in his chest, the elusive memories that danced on the periphery of her consciousness, proven by her nightmares. He clenched his jaw, torn between the skepticism that came with his profession and the unwavering pull of an inexplicable bond. "Julie," he murmured, the name reverberating in the confines of his office.

He returned to the file on the Revivalists. Catamount focused on the information, his detective instincts driving him to piece together the puzzle. Yet an undercurrent of something tugged at him—a tug fueled by a belief that Juliette might just hold the key to bringing down the murdering bastards.

"Captain," Bradley said, interrupting his contemplation, "we're making progress on the rest of the journal, but that Lord Arnold was a confusing weasel. It's taking time to decipher his notes."

Catamount nodded, pushing his personal concerns to the background, at least for the moment. "I want every detail on their recent movements that he wrote down. We need to anticipate their next move."

As Bradley left, Catamount's gaze lingered on the file, but his mind spiraled back to Juliette. The notion that she might be his long-lost Julie simmered beneath the surface, an unresolved chord that vibrated within him. And the idea that she might be hiding, that she didn't trust him enough to reveal herself, added a layer of worry and frustration.

He paced his office, the creaking floorboards beneath his boots evidence of his restless agitation. "Damn it, Julie," he muttered. "I'm certain it's her. Why doesn't she come forward? Why the charade?" He raked his hands through his disheveled hair, the gold-tipped strands slipping through his fingers like grains of sand. "What are you hiding from?" he wondered aloud.

As he circled his office, he considered the implications. "Is she running from danger, or is she playing some awful game? No, she wouldn't do that." Still, unease settled deep within him at that possibility. "I've seen enough deceit in this city. Can't escape it, can I? If she's Julie, what's she afraid of? And if she's not…" His thoughts trailed off, the uncertainty gnawing at him like an unrelenting dog on a bone. "Some days I think I'm just making this whole bloody thing up."

With a last, lingering look at the scattered clues on his desk, Catamount refocused on the case, determined to pierce through the fog of mystery surrounding Juliette and the looming threat of the Revivalists.

Several minutes later, the door creaked open again, and Catamount's eyes snapped from the scattered reports on his desk. There she was—Juliette, a vision that struck him like a bolt of lightning and sent a shock wave through his chest. She'd changed and was now in a burgundy dress that clung to her incredible figure. She moved with a hurried grace, and her auburn hair framed her face in loose tendrils. Her freckles—those that dusted her nose and cheeks in the same delicate pattern as Julie's—stood out against her creamy skin.

A blast of emotion hit him, and for a moment, he stood frozen. Then, instinctively, his arms opened wide, drawn by an unseen force. He didn't understand it. He just did it. Opened them wide for this woman, knowing without knowing that it was what she needed.

Juliette, emotion shimmering in her beautiful eyes, rushed into his embrace. The reports and investigations were forgotten with her in his arms.

Without words they met in a collision of passion, a union of force and feeling that left them both breathless. Her lips moved against his, familiar and yet new. He tasted the traces of shared history on her lips, mingled with secrets that hung in the air. For a moment, the weight of duty melted away, and there was only the sensation of Juliette in his arms.

It was a wholly unexpected kiss, and a rush of emotions swept through him. Juliette's actions were cryptic, and lost in the heat of the moment he couldn't decipher them. The tangle of his emotions and any questions evaporated with each tug of her fingers in his hair. Juliette's mews drowned in the intensity of their kisses, a cascade of desire that flared wildly. He yielded to the magnetic pull of her lips, forgetting the questions that had plagued his thoughts only moments before.

Her actions spoke louder than any words, and in that moment, explanations seemed trivial. Who needed them when he had her warm and willing in his arms? Catamount's resistance crumbled, and he kissed her back with every bit of feeling he'd shoved deep down and pushed aside. It came roaring out, expressed through tongue and lips and hard, searching hands.

Juliette's breathy voice cut through the haze as she yanked away. "I couldn't stay away any longer," she confessed between kisses, her hands still firmly entangled in his hair.

He managed to pull back just enough to mutter, "What's going on?"

She silenced him with another kiss, her reply muffled against his lips. "I couldn't resist you any longer. I needed to feel your touch, your kiss. I know I'm not making any sense after the way I rushed out this morning. And I went walking and realized that it's *you*. I… I need you, Catamount."

The questions that had plagued his mind moments ago were replaced with the demanding pulse of desire. He whispered, "Whatever brought you here, I'm not letting you go again."

"Good," she growled, grasping a fistful of his linen shirt,

"don't." Her lips sought his once again, urgent and verging on frantic.

"Wait," he murmured, loving her taste but pulling away with mountainous effort.

"No more waiting." Her lips took his again—those full, sensual lips he knew so well from a lifetime ago.

Resistance was nonexistent.

He was lost.

"*Julie.*" Every bit of him lit up with love and need for his woman—*this* woman who knew not who she truly was. But he did.

Perhaps he should show her.

Grasping at her with hungry hands, Catamount traced her curves, reveled in their feel. "Damn, you fill my hands so right," he rasped, cupping her breasts before yanking impatiently at the bodice of her dress. "So very right." Her breasts sprang free, and a need so big, so violent, swept through him that he nearly lost control right then and there.

Juliette gasped and dropped her head back, exposing the long column of her throat. "Why—" she started, and cut off on a moan when his mouth covered her nipple and his tongue washed over the delectable peak. "Oh, don't stop," she demanded, burrowing her hands into his hair and holding him to her. "This... this feels... *Oh!*" she cried out when he nipped at her playfully, arching into him.

"I know you like that." Because his Julie did. In fact, she also liked...

"Oh my God!" Juliette groaned and melted against him as he stroked his tongue, bold and possessive, across her peak. Over and over, making her arch impossibly into him.

Knowing her body, even as she didn't yet remember, Catamount brought his thumb to her other peak and began flicking in time with his tongue. If she was indeed his Julie, the combination would shatter her. Christ, he loved how sensitive her breasts were, had always been. Having this additional way to take her over the edge had always pleased him in the most primal way. "Hold on to me, love," he said with dark satisfaction, his breath brushing across her skin. "You're about to touch stars."

With single-minded intent, Catamount built her up, bringing her closer and closer to the crest with his mouth and hands, loving her breasts with open hunger. With every flick of his tongue, his heart thumped a thunderous beat of love and belonging, of passion for this exquisite woman in his arms.

"Cat!" she called out, her nails digging into his shoulders.

He grunted with pleasure—at the nearness of her orgasm and at her use of his nickname. "That's the way, love. Just like that."

She came, splintering apart in his arms.

How he'd craved that. *Fuck*, how he'd craved that. "More," he commanded, ready to give her as many as she could take.

But then... a tear. He felt it spatter gently against his skin, warm and wet. Alarm rang in his mind. No, he hadn't pushed too far and hurt her? Christ, he couldn't bear that if he had. "Juliette?" He raised his head to look at her. "Did I... did I hurt you?"

"No," she whispered, swiping at her face with the back of her hand, her mass of auburn hair tumbling about her as she shook her head. "I just... I'm not myself right now."

She'd been exquisitely herself, to his way of thinking.

"I'm sorry, love." He gently recomposed her bodice, tenderly tucking her modestly within. "Can I do anything?"

"Hold me, *s'il vous plaît*," she said as she melted into his embrace, seeming to take comfort there. "Just hold me."

As if letting go was an option.

CHAPTER FOURTEEN

BOND STREET, ELEGANT with its high-end boutiques, lay shrouded in an eerie stillness as Juliette and Catamount approached her shop later that evening. The street lamps flickered, casting elongated shadows on the cobblestone streets. Her heart raced, a sense of foreboding gripping her as she neared her establishment.

The door to the shop hung ajar. Catamount tensed beside her, his instincts as a seasoned detective clearly on high alert. The scent of something unfamiliar hung in the air, an unsettling perfume that assaulted their senses. Upon crossing the threshold, the disarray inside became painfully apparent. Fabrics were strewn across the floor, dress forms toppled over like fallen soldiers, and shattered glass from broken display cases sparkled in the dim light. It was a terrible scene, a violation of the sanctuary Juliette had painstakingly created.

Her breath hitched as she surveyed the wreckage. *"Mon Dieu, what happened here?"* she whispered, her voice tinged with disbelief and sorrow.

Catamount scanned the scene, his jaw tightening. "Looks like someone was searching for something. Deliberately tearing the place apart."

Her fingers fluttered to her chest as she clutched the pendant around her neck. "What could they be searching for?" Her gaze met Catamount's, eyes wide with desperation.

He crouched to inspect the damage, running a gloved hand over the fabric strewn across the floor. "They weren't just searching for any trinket, Juliette. This was a targeted act. I'm certain it's connected to the Revivalists."

The weight of his words settled heavily on her shoulders. "But why? What could they want here? With me?"

Catamount rose to his full height, seriousness etched into his features. "You tell me."

She saw the fury brewing within Catamount like a tempest as he surveyed the wreckage of her shop. His hands clenched into fists with a rage that clearly simmered just beneath the surface. Her violated space, the destruction wrought upon her carefully curated store, ignited a fire within him. "Damn them," he muttered through gritted teeth, scanning the disarray with an intensity that could pierce through steel. The Bow Street Runner in him took in the scene, noted everything. She watched him work, amazed.

Observing the controlled fury in Catamount's eyes, Juliette was reassured. His protective instincts, though fierce, were a source of solace in the face of the unknown threat. She stepped closer to him. "We'll find who did this," she whispered, her voice steady despite the shakiness within.

His gaze shifted to hers, a storm of emotions in the piercing green. His curses resonated through the space as he looked around. Drawers were pulled open, belongings scattered, and the air was tinged with the acrid scent of pipe smoke.

"They were looking for something, Juliette," Catamount growled, the veins in his neck pulsing with anger. "This wasn't just a random act. What are you hiding? What is it that you haven't been telling me this whole bloody time?"

"Nothing," she mumbled, mostly believing it. She gripped the edge of a nearby table to steady herself. "I'm not hiding anything, and I've done nothing to warrant their attention."

"Oh, you're hiding something, all right," Catamount scoffed, his frustration palpable. "A whole damned lot of something.

Christ, I wish you'd trust me."

Juliette's conscience pricked at his words, her eyes narrowing as she observed the wreckage around them. What were they searching for? What did they want from her? She moved toward her office in the back, taking it all in. "They left me nothing unharmed."

"We need to figure out what they were after," Catamount said, his determination burning bright in his eyes.

"Catamount?" she said as she entered her office and came to an abrupt stop.

"What is it?"

"I-I think it's a message from the Revivalists."

"Shite," he growled, and was beside her in an instant. She pointed to the ominous message scrawled on her wall.

Give it to us.

The ink, a dark proclamation of danger, pulsed with a malevolent energy.

Catamount cursed under his breath. "They're sending a message, Juliette," he gritted out. "This is personal."

Her heart thumped painfully fast. The room was suffocating as the weight of the threat hung in the air. "Catamount, why are they doing this to me?" Her voice quivered.

"They want something you have, or they believe you know something crucial," he replied. "We need to find out what it is before they come back." His eyes never wavered from the message on the wall, his mind clearly calculating the next move as he paced the room, his agitation palpable. "Dammit, Juliette! This is a direct threat, a blatant escalation. They've crossed a line."

She stood by the damaged furniture. "I don't have anything they could want. And I won't be a pawn in their game, Catamount."

His gaze suddenly softened, the intensity of his protective rage giving way to a more tender concern. "I don't want you to get hurt. I can't lose you again."

The way he said *again*… She almost believed it.

"We need answers," he continued. "The Revivalists won't stop until they get what they want. And I won't rest until they're brought to justice."

He pulled her close, his lips crashing against hers in a fierce, demanding kiss. Juliette felt a swirl of arousal, the heat of his lips both comforting and electrifying. But no sooner had she thrown her hands around his neck for anchorage, he broke apart from her, breathless. "I won't let them hurt you. Not again," he declared.

Then he pushed away and paced the ransacked flat like a caged tiger, his frustration manifesting in a low growl. "Grab your essentials. You're staying with me," he ordered her, his voice brooking no argument.

She blinked in astonishment, caught off guard by the unexpected plan. "I appreciate your concern, but I can't just abandon my shop—"

He cut her off with a sharp gesture. "This is about your safety, Juliette. The Revivalists won't hesitate to target you again. I won't allow it." As she stood there, grappling with a sudden whirlwind of emotions, he stepped closer. "You don't have a choice in this. Pack what you need. We're leaving."

The authority in his voice resonated, and despite the mess surrounding them, there was an odd sense of security in his command. Juliette hesitated for a moment before nodding, her own resolve firming. "Only if you cook for me."

"Every damn day for the rest of your life. Done." He didn't even blink.

Him? Cook for her? *Every single day.* And he agreed without hesitation?

Wow. Simply wow.

She looked up at him through her lashes. "You would do that for me?"

He kissed her. Hard and fervent and so deep she felt him clear to her soul as she clung to him.

Juliette whispered against his lips, "Fine. Your place it is."
"Good." anchorage
"But we take my kitten."

CHAPTER FIFTEEN

"I HAD NO idea you lived so luxuriously." Juliette glanced around Catamount's Belgravia flat, silently impressed. In her mind, world-weary detectives lived in dark, cramped flats with stacks of dusty files one moderate breeze away from toppling into a scrambled mess on the ground. At least, she had believed that until ten minutes ago, when she'd followed him into his flat and her jaw had dropped at the sight.

"I'll give you a tour later," he said before rounding on her and pinning her to the front door, his large, hard body flush against the length of her. "But first, this."

"Oh my," she breathed, liking the feel of him. So hot. So powerful.

"Julie," he murmured, lowering his head as he nuzzled the spot at the base of her neck.

Awareness shot through her. "What are you doing?"

"Kissing your neck, is that all right?" His lips left a tingling trail in their wake.

It was more than all right. It was wonderful. Like something she knew intimately and cherished with all her heart. "Don't stop," she whispered.

"I wasn't planning to." His hands slid around her waist and pulled her more firmly against him.

"Thank you for today," she said, thinking of all the hard work he'd put in to make her safe. "I think you did your men proud."

"Yeah? That's good," he said as his hands began to roam leisurely over her body. They stroked up her hips and ribcage, the tips of his fingers just brushing the underside of her breasts. They plumped and began to ache, eager for his touch. The way he touched her felt both familiar and new. It was an arousing combination.

Catamount was making it hard for her to concentrate on what he was saying. "What did you say?"

"You feel damned good in my hands." Amusement laced his voice as he repeated himself.

Oh. "I feel like I belong in them."

"You do belong." He cupped her breasts, making her gasp softly. "You belong right here with me."

Arousal coursed through her, turning her veins to molten gold. She raised her hands and looped her fingers loosely around his neck. "I want to be here, Catamount," she whispered, meaning it. There was no place in the world she would rather be. Only right here in his arms.

In the window on the far side of the room, their reflection caught her eye. As she watched, his large hands covered her breasts, his thumbs brushing across her puckered nipples. His head was lowered and shimmered rich bronze in the play of firelight. He had the most beautiful hair she'd ever seen. He was beautiful, period.

And you've never, ever stopped loving him, her heart whispered, ripping a gasp from her throat.

Now it was time to show him.

CATAMOUNT FELT THE moment when Juliette made the decision to welcome him because her body melted against his. Excellent, because he'd already made her his own. Juliette belonged with him. Always had. He couldn't wait any longer to show her.

Releasing her breasts, he slipped his hands underneath her skirts and discovered the smooth, warm skin beneath. "I want to see all of you."

"According to you, you already have," she whispered back.

"Not like this I haven't." He'd never seen *Juliette* naked with the firelight from his flat's fireplace dancing across her dips and curves. And it was Juliette who was making him feel so much that he needed to do something about it now or he was going to explode.

Impatience bared its teeth, and Catamount knew it was time. After everything he'd felt today, there was no turning back from this. He needed Juliette. Maybe he'd always needed her.

Gripping her dress in his hands, he pulled it over her head and threw it on the hardwood floor. Then he made quick work of her corset. Her breasts sprang free, and he groaned at the gorgeousness, watching them sway gently before him. They were exactly how he remembered them.

Catamount reached for the waistband of her linen drawers. Very slowly he drew the flap open, pure male satisfaction filling him at the wide-eyed, aroused look he could see on her face. When he dipped his fingers inside, she bit her lip and moaned, rocking against his hand.

Desire ripped through him, destroying any last bit of restraint. "Juliette," he growled, and pushed his hand further down her drawers. When he reached her hot pussy, he slipped a finger between her slick folds and discovered how wet she already was for him.

Mine.

"Come for me," he demanded, wanting to see her face as she orgasmed on his hand again. Catamount needed to watch as she surrendered to the way he made her feel. How *they* made each other feel.

Finding her center, he began rubbing the swollen bud in slow circles, just the way he knew she loved. Possessiveness flooded him. Juliette loved the way he touched her. *Only him.*

"Catamount!" she gasped, and leaned her head back against his shoulder, her eyes closed. He could feel her hips moving restlessly against him, and it spurred him on. Made him hungry for more.

"That's it, love," he urged, moving his finger more purposefully on her now. "Come for me."

Her body began to tremble with impending release. Feeling how close she was, Catamount took his free hand and cupped a breast, plucking gently at her nipple. As he watched her in the window reflection, she moaned and whimpered, losing herself in the feel. With a throaty groan, she came all over his hand.

It was the most gorgeous fucking thing he'd ever seen.

Lowering them to the thick Persian rug in front of the roaring fire, Catamount quickly stripped off his clothes. "That was gorgeous," he said, then kissed Juliette long and deep once they were both lying naked on the rug. "You're gorgeous. Now give me more."

She gave him a thoroughly satisfied look. "I'm not sure I have another one in me."

"Want to bet?"

He found her slick entrance and pushed fully inside her, groaning at the hot, tight feel. She moaned too, and pulled her knees up, taking him even deeper. "Maybe I have one more."

Catamount made sure she did. Thrusting into her slowly at first, he kept up the gentle pace until she began to writhe underneath him. Until she closed her eyes in ecstasy.

Then he lost control.

He dropped to his elbows and cradled her head in his hands. Pumping hard, he let himself go. Let himself express everything he couldn't say. Every thrust, every touch, every kiss showed her how he felt. Juliette belonged to him. His woman. His love.

When her inner muscles began to squeeze around him in impending orgasm, Catamount lowered his forehead to hers, "That's it, darling," he said, and kept stroking deep, over and over until she cried out in blissful surrender again, her body milking him to his own release. He came hard then, seeing stars, his body shaking.

Holy shite.

CHAPTER SIXTEEN

EARLY LIGHT SEEPED through the curtains the next morning, casting a soft glow over Catamount's flat. For a moment, she listened to the deep, rhythmic breathing next to her, loving the sound. Smiling to herself as she gently slipped out of bed, careful not to disturb her sleeping detective, she padded into the huge kitchen wearing only her shift that she'd grabbed from the floor on her way.

The aroma of black tea filled the air as she found a jar and opened it. A kettle perched on the stove nearby, and the soft hiss of the flame sounded as she lit it. Odette wound around her ankles, a comforting presence in the silent room. "Ah, *mon ami*, look at the two of us. Temporarily homeless, we are. What shall we do about these blasted Revivalists so that we can get our home and shop back?" she mused, bending down to stroke the kitten's fluffy fur. Odette purred in response and stretched into her hand, seeming to not mind her fancy new surroundings.

Juliette poured hot water into the waiting teapot, the fragrant leaves unfurling as they steeped. As the room filled with the soothing aroma, she settled into a chair, cradling her cup in her hands. "They think they can terrorize me. *Non*, they cannot," she whispered to Odette, who blinked up at her with curious eyes. "I am made of stronger character than that."

Juliette's mind raced with ideas on how to capture the murdering madmen, each plan more daring and outrageous than the last. If she was serious about catching them and putting an end to all this, then she needed to outwit the Revivalists, to turn the tables on those who sought to plunge her world into oblivion. But could she? Could she really do it?

Could she, Juliette Toussaint, mere modiste, plot against the Revivalists?

Her. Not Catamount, though his presence was a godsend. Not the Bow Street Runners. Not anyone but her.

She glanced toward her bedchamber door to where Catamount slept in the bed beyond. The protection he offered fueled her resolve, but she knew she needed a plan—something cunning and unexpected. Because Catamount was right—it was personal with the Revivalists. They wanted her and whatever was locked up tight in her mind.

They wanted what she couldn't remember.

Tea in hand, she leaned back, staring out of the kitchen window into the dawn-painted sky. Odette curled up on the windowsill.

"We shall bring them to justice, *mon ami*, and ensure they rue the day they crossed paths with Juliette Toussaint," she told her feline confidante. The kitten didn't stir. "No? Well, perhaps I'll think on it anyway." Juliette lost herself in thoughts of strategy. The quiet of the early morning cocooned her in a semblance of peace. Yet beneath the tranquil surface lurked the very real threat of the Revivalists.

As she absently stroked her kitten's fur, a sudden, unbidden flood of visions surged through her mind, tearing through the carefully erected barriers she had built to protect herself from such things. The scent of smoke, the distant cries of distress, and the ominous shadows of Seven Dials painted a vivid picture in her mind, overtaking all her senses.

She saw it.

That fateful night when the Revivalists struck—it tormented her mind.

In the kitchen, the clinking of her teacup against the saucer ceased to be heard by her ears, the sound replaced by the ghostly echoes of distant screams.

"No! Please, don't hurt them!" The cry reverberated through the corridors of her memory as she screamed it out loud into the silence of the kitchen. "Stop! Let them go!"

She could feel the rough cobblestone beneath her fingertips, the tremors of fear coursing through her veins as she huddled against the alley wall. The memories, long buried, clawed their way back into her consciousness. Took her by violent, vicious storm. Turned her upside down and inside out.

They *hurt*.

"Juliette!" A distant voice called her name, calling her back to the present. "Juliette, it's Catamount. Can you hear me? Come on, love." Somewhere she vaguely registered Odette nuzzled against her hand, sensing her distress. "Listen to my voice."

The weight of the past pressed upon her like an unbearable burden, and she slumped against the kitchen table. The cold surface seemed to yank her back into the present, but the darkness and pain of that night clawed at her, threatening to pull her right back under. Ugly, greedy memories, they were.

A soft whimper escaped her lips. "*Non*, not again," she muttered as she felt them overtaking her mind once more.

"Juliette, what's happening?" Catamount's voice, laden with concern, cut through the painful haze. She could tell he had entered the kitchen—his presence felt solid and strong.

Tears welled in Juliette's eyes as she struggled through visions to find the words. "The Revivalists... They attacked Seven Dials. So much pain, so much blood. I couldn't save them. Oh, Catamount, I couldn't save those people!"

"You're not alone, Juliette. You have me. And you're stronger than you know."

As he wrapped his arms around her, the warmth of his embrace began to chip away at the icy tendrils the past held around her heart and mind. Little Odette, sensing the shift, hopped into her lap and nestled against her, offering her silent support.

Juliette looked up, blinking blurry eyes.

Catamount stood beside her, comforting her in the aftermath of the terrorizing memories more than he could possibly know. His touch on her shoulder was a grounding force. "Julie," he whispered.

Juliette, enveloped in his strong arms, felt a shiver run down her spine at the sound of the endearing name. It held a familiarity, a tenderness that spoke volumes. "Catamount," she replied.

His lips brushed against her forehead in a gentle, lingering kiss, a gesture filled with both comfort and desire. "You don't have to hide from the past anymore," he murmured against her skin, the warmth of his breath sending a shiver through her.

She tilted her head up to meet his gaze, drawn into the depths of his pale green eyes. The golden-tipped bronze of his hair caught the soft light filtering through the curtains, giving him an almost angelic glow. Yet his rugged features and the world-weary energy that clung to him spoke of the battles he'd fought on the callous streets of London.

"I don't intend to," she confessed, her eyes locking on to his.

Catamount's lips claimed hers in a deep, drugging kiss. The world outside their embrace seemed to fade, leaving only the quiet breaths they shared. "Let's face all these demons together," he whispered against her lips. "The ones in your head and the ones on the streets."

As Catamount held her close, Juliette noticed the ease with which he cradled her in his arms. There was an undeniable familiarity, a seamless connection that spoke of a deeper understanding between them. Like he navigated the contours of her body with an innate knowledge, an intimacy that went beyond the physical. His touch, strong and sure, seemed to trace invisible lines across her, leaving a trail of warmth in its wake. The gentle pressure of his embrace felt like a custom fit, tailored to the curves and angles of her body. It was as if he truly knew her, intimately, down to the very essence of her. His touch, the way he held her, was more than comforting—it was a language of shared history and experiences. The soft press of his lips against her forehead, the gentle caress of his fingers on her skin, all spoke of a connection that transcended the present.

"Julie," he whispered. As Catamount's arms enveloped her, Juliette noticed a subtle shift within herself. The name *Julie* no longer carried the weight of unfamiliarity; instead, it offered a sense of comfort, a strength that she instinctively leaned into. "Julie," he murmured again, the endearment now a whispered reassurance. In response, she snuggled deeper into his embrace, finding solace in the familiarity of the name and the security of his arms.

"I remember a night, years ago," he began. "We were in the countryside, the air crisp with the scent of autumn. The moonlight spilled across the fields, and you"—he paused, a soft smile playing on his lips—"you laughed like I'd never heard before."

"Tell me," she encouraged him.

"There was a bonfire, and you danced under the stars," he continued, his voice tinged with affection. "You were carefree, untamed. It was a moment etched in my mind—one of those rare instances when the weight of the world seemed to lift."

A wistful smile curved her lips as she listened to the intimate recollection. The lines between the present Juliette and the past Julie blurred momentarily, a glimpse into a life that held shared laughter and stolen moments beneath the vast night sky.

Catamount's arms tightened around her, as if to anchor them both in the present. "I miss that Julie," he admitted, his gaze holding a depth of emotion as he looked down at her. "But I'm grateful for every moment with you, Juliette, whatever memories we may share from now into the future."

⇥⟫⟪⇤

THE AROMA OF freshly brewed tea wafted through the air, enveloping Catamount's flat. The large space, decorated with antique furniture and maps from his past cases, carried an air of rugged charm. Juliette, sitting at the table, observed him with amusement and appreciation as he prepared his own cup.

"So, the fierce detective makes a mean cup of tea," Juliette teased, a playful smile gracing her lips.

He chuckled. "Years of practice. You can't navigate the underbelly of London without mastering the art of tea making. Too many late nights slogging over reports, searching for evidence and clues. Tea keeps you going."

Juliette, sipping her tea, appreciated the juxtaposition of the masculine detective performing domestic tasks. "You're quite the paradox. A hardened detective with a penchant for brewing a comforting cup of tea."

He raised an eyebrow, a spark of humor in his pale green eyes. "Life is full of surprises."

As they settled into their cups of tea, the discussion veered toward the day's plans. He was determined to keep her safe, and proposed her spending the day at Bow Street.

But her priorities lay with salvaging the remnants of her ransacked shop. "I can't spend the day at Bow Street headquarters and just leave my shop in ruins," she protested.

He sighed, clearly recognizing the stubborn resolve in her eyes. "I want you safe. Bow Street is the best place for now. We can deal with the shop later."

She leaned back in the armchair. "What if I just stay here and promise not to leave your flat for any reason?"

He regarded her for several long, silent moments, exasperation evident. "Christ, you're a handful. Fine, but you better keep that promise."

With a victorious grin, Juliette agreed. The negotiation settled, she again marveled at the hominess of the morning. Like they'd done it a million times already.

After finishing his cup in companionable and easy silence, Catamount stood from the table and prepared to leave for Bow Street. The scent of freshly brewed tea still lingered, as well as the cozy feeling of domesticity. However, unbeknownst to Catamount, a quiet determination burned in Juliette's gut as she watched him ready for the day.

As he fastened the buttons of his crisp shirt, she bit back guilt, knowing that she intended to slip away as soon as he stepped out the door. While musing with Odette earlier over how to catch the Revivalists, she'd had an idea. Now it was urgent that she speak to Catamount's sister Carenza and his sister-in-law Sadie—two people who'd survived their attacks and whom she knew from dressing at her shop. She hoped in talking to them she would find answers and insights into the Revivalist attacks, learn of a weakness she could exploit.

She knew the risk in keeping her plan a secret. Catamount would undoubtedly insist she accompany him to Bow Street if he knew she wished to go seeking answers on her own. But she couldn't help it. After those awful visions, she knew deep down that she needed the wisdom of those who had also endured the Revivalists' brutality before.

As Catamount adjusted the collar of his coat, Juliette feigned a smile, concealing the conflicting emotions that churned beneath her surface. Was it so bad that she wanted to protect him—the man she cared for? Even if he was a detective. After last night and what passed between them, he was also her person. Her love. Seeking knowledge that might help ensure their survival and capture the Revivalists seemed wise to her. A good and right thing to do.

"Off to the office?" she asked, injecting casual cheer into her voice. Once she'd learned what she hoped to from his female relatives, then she'd share with him. But she couldn't learn anything if she stayed locked in his flat all day.

Catamount nodded, the familiar seriousness settling into his features. "Yes, love. I need to check in and see if there are any leads on the Revivalists, report your shop break-in. You'll truly stay here, won't you?"

She tossed him a reassuring smile. "Of course. I'll be right here, safe and sound."

As he pressed a quick kiss to her forehead, she forced her thoughts away from the guilt niggling her. He let her go and stepped to the entrance, reaching for the doorknob, ready to step into the day's challenges. "Wait," she called after him.

Her hand shot out, grabbing his with an urgency that halted his departure. He turned to face her, and was met with a sudden, passionate hug. In a whirlwind of emotions, Juliette flung herself into his arms, her lips seeking his in a fervent kiss.

Caught off guard, Catamount rocked back on his feet, quickly surrendering to the moment, pulling her close as she kissed him hard. For a brief, suspended moment, the danger she was in disappeared. The scent of tea, the soft glow of morning light, and the warmth of their entwined bodies took over her senses. And she reveled in it—*needed* it. Needed to forget the fear and just be in the moment with the man who made her heart sing.

When they finally broke apart, breathless, Catamount's eyes locked on to hers. As he caressed her cheek, a gentle smile played on his lips. "Take care, Julie," he whispered.

Juliette nodded. "You too, Catamount." Why was there a lump in her throat? This wasn't their last parting! Why was she acting like such a ninny?

With a final, lingering glance at her, Catamount stepped out into the day, leaving her heart pounding with the thrill of their stolen moment and the daunting challenges that awaited her.

The door clicked shut behind him, leaving her alone in the quiet flat. She turned toward her tiny companion perched on the windowsill. With a sly smile, she rubbed her hands together, a gesture more reflective of her nerves than any cunning. "All right, my sweet girl," she addressed Odette, who blinked up at her with curiosity. "We've got a plan to hatch and noblewomen to track down."

Odette just kept blinking round eyes at her.

"Fine, I know what you're thinking, and yes, it is a bit under-handed. Perhaps even misleading, not telling him about my true intentions for the day. But it's only temporary, and I will absolutely tell him anything I find out. Anything at all that's relevant. So, you can stop looking at me like that."

Juliette shot the kitten a defensive glance and began pacing around the room. Her mind raced with thoughts and strategies. There was a certain thrill with taking matters into her own hands. Was that how Catamount felt each time he investigated a case?

"I'm going to find those ladies," she declared to Odette. "They've faced the Revivalists before, and I need their wisdom. Catamount might not like it, but it's happening."

She approached the window where the morning light spilled into the room and her kitten sat. "I'll be back before he returns," she assured Odette, gently brushing her fur. "He'll never even know."

But she couldn't stand the silent judgment in her kitten's eyes, so found parchment and hastily scribbled a note. "There. Happy now?"

Odette purred and curled into a tiny ball on the windowsill.

With a final glance around Catamount's flat, Juliette slipped out the door, her guilty heart pounding in her chest.

CHAPTER SEVENTEEN

As Juliette stepped out onto Belgrave Square, the crisp November air greeted her, carrying with it the mingling scents of autumn leaves and distant chimney smoke. The fashionable denizens of Belgravia, wrapped in layers of luxurious fabrics, strolled past the high-end boutiques and shops and homes. Despite the urgency in her step, she couldn't help but notice the vibrant display of colors from the changing leaves and the elegant clothing of the *ton*.

As she made her way through the thoroughfare, a gentle breeze whisked fallen leaves around her ankles. A street vendor peddling roasted chestnuts called out, "Fresh chestnuts, miss? Warm your hands and your heart!"

Juliette smiled, declining the offer with a gracious shake of her head. "No, thank you!"

Her fine rose silk gown, though slightly out of place, garnered approving glances from passersby. A well-dressed couple stopped her for a moment, complimenting her attire. "Your gown is exquisite! A creation from your own hands?" the lady inquired.

Juliette inclined her head, grinning. "Indeed, it is. *Merci* for the compliment."

The gentleman, intrigued, added, "Do you have a shop near-by? I'm certain my wife would love to explore your creations."

As Juliette explained the location of her modiste shop on Bond Street, a twinge of sadness crept in, given the state it was currently in. She would restore it—she would. And she'd start as soon as she was done with this task.

The sun cast long shadows on the cobbled streets as Juliette approached Grosvenor Square. Tall, elegant townhouses framed the square, each exuding opulence and refinement. The sunlight filtered through the branches of ancient trees, casting dappled shadows on the cobblestone paths. Carriages rolled by, their wheels creating a rhythmic clatter on the cobbles.

Her destination, Tipton House, the grandest residence on the square, loomed ahead. Its imposing façade, adorned with intricate carvings and tall windows, spoke of generations of aristocratic splendor. A wrought-iron gate with the Tipton family crest welcomed guests into the opulent home beyond.

Nerves fluttered in her stomach as she approached. Tipton House was the residence of the Duchess of Seawell and her husband, Lord Castlebury, Catamount's brother. It was also the home of the dowager countess, a lady she had adorned with several gowns over the past three years. The societal hierarchy of London added an extra layer of formality to the visit, and Juliette's finely tuned modiste instincts urged her to ensure a favorable impression.

The scent of blooming flowers greeted her as she stepped onto the perfectly manicured grounds. The vibrant hues of the garden contrasted with the muted tones of the surrounding buildings, creating a picturesque scene. Juliette's eyes darted around, taking in every detail—the symmetrical layout, the carefully tended topiaries, and the occasional rustling of leaves in the gentle breeze. Approaching the grand entrance, she hesitated for a moment. The brass knocker on the imposing door gleamed in the sunlight, and she took a deep breath, gathering her resolve.

With a firm tap of the knocker, the sound echoed through the square. Moments later, the door swung open, revealing the elegant foyer of Tipton House. A footman in black and white livery stood at attention, his expression impassive as he awaited her announcement.

She offered a polite smile and announced herself. "I am Madame Juliette Toussaint, seeking an audience with the Her Grace Sadie Castlebury, Duchess of Seawell. I bring tidings and hope for a moment of her gracious consideration." With any luck at all, Lady Carenza would also be at Tipton House.

The footman, trained in the art of discretion, nodded and ushered her inside. The scent of polished wood and fresh flowers enveloped her as she stepped into the vestibule. Polished wood floors gleamed underfoot, and the richly detailed painting on the walls hinted at the storied history within the grand residence.

At that moment, Lady Carenza stepped into the foyer. Glossy golden curls cascaded around her shoulders, and sapphire-blue eyes sparkled with warmth as she approached. "Juliette! *Mon ami!*" Lady Carenza exclaimed. She wrapped Juliette in a warm hug, a gesture that spoke of their years of friendship. "It's been too long, *cherie*. I've missed your laughter in these halls," Carenza continued, holding Juliette at arm's length to take in her appearance. "And what a vision you are! The gown, the hair— simply exquisite." She linked arms with Juliette, leading her further into the residence. "Come, let us find a comfortable spot. I'm positively eager to catch up. It has been too long since I've visited your shop, shame on me. How have you been?"

As they walked through the lavish corridors, ease settled over Juliette. Lady Carenza's genuine enthusiasm and the familiarity of the surroundings reassured her, making Tipton House feel more like a haven than a place of incredible status and wealth.

The drawing room, in soothing shades of blue, welcomed them as Lady Carenza led Juliette to a pair of elegantly upholstered chairs. The air carried the faint scent of freshly brewed tea as a maid arranged a silver tray with delicate cups and saucers.

The viscountess settled onto one of the chairs, her eyes brimming with curiosity. "Now, tell me, what brings you to Tipton House today?"

Juliette took the other seat. "I come seeking wisdom of a very personal nature. Troubles have found their way to my doorstep, and I thought of no better confidantes than the Castlebury ladies who have faced these monsters themselves."

Lady Carenza's mouth flopped open in shock, but before she could respond, the door opened, and the duchess entered, her sharp green eyes assessing the scene with a knowing glint. Her rich, dark brown hair framed her face, and her petite, fit build exuded a quiet strength. A genuine smile of warmth spread across her features as she greeted Juliette. "It's been too long! What a delightful surprise," she exclaimed, crossing the room.

The maid, attentive to her role, poured fragrant tea into delicate cups. The gentle clink of porcelain added a melodic note to the atmosphere as the women settled into the comfort of the drawing room.

"I hope you don't mind the intrusion," Juliette began, her eyes shifting between the women.

Sadie, with a reassuring smile, gestured toward the tea. "No intrusion at all. We're friends. We're more than happy to offer whatever aid we can. Now, let's share a cup of tea and discuss how we might be of help."

Juliette settled back into the plush chair with her tea, uncertain how and where to begin. Perhaps it was best simply to dive right in. "It's a long, complicated story, but I'll summarize the best that I can." Raising the delicate cup to her lips, she took a soothing sip. "For the past three years I've been haunted by nightmares, visions of a night that I've recently come to realize is Seven Dials from when the Revivalists attacked. Do you remember that? It was in all the papers."

The ladies nodded.

"During the attack, I believe I suffered a head injury. Since then, I can't remember anything from my life before that night," Juliette confessed, her voice carrying the weight of the unspoken fear that had lingered in the shadows of her consciousness. "Truly. I woke in an alley in Covent Garden covered in blood from a wound in my head, a carpetbag in my hands. And I had no idea how I'd gotten there. I knew nothing about the bag in my hand or where I lived. I just sat there and cried for what felt like hours. Until I looked at the callouses on my fingers and realized that I must be a seamstress. I stood up, wiped my face with the torn and singed remnants of my dress, and went on from there."

Carenza and Sadie exchanged glances, their expressions a mix of concern and surprise. The revelation held a gravity that seeped into the very fabric of the room.

"I've lost three years of my life, and with it, all the memories, the people I knew, and the person I used to be," Juliette continued, her fingers tracing an absent pattern on the arm of the chair. "I've been grappling with fragments of a past that eludes me, and it's tearing at the edges of my sanity." A sudden realization flickered in her mind. She leaned forward. "Wait a moment. You both know Catamount. You know him well. Did he tell you about me? About a woman named Julie?"

Carenza and Sadie exchanged puzzled glances before turning back to Juliette.

"Catamount? Are you serious? We're privy to nothing private about that man. He's a brick wall of silence," Carenza scoffed.

"I assumed… I thought that perhaps, through Catamount, you might have known me before my memory loss. That maybe he had spoken of our connection. The one he keeps insisting we have. He tells me I'm a woman named Julie, not Juliette."

Sadie shook her head. "Catamount is a private man. Your past with him, if you have one, is a mystery to us."

Lady Carenza's brow furrowed as she processed Juliette's revelation. "Wait, why can't you remember? Could hitting your head have caused such a loss of memory?"

Juliette took a deep breath, her gaze drifting to the window. "I think it might have triggered some form of amnesia. But that's not the only problem. There's more to the story, something I'm missing. It's brought the Revivalists back to haunt me." As she poured out her fears, a terrible vulnerability gripped her voice. "What if I don't remember everything because I don't want to? What if there's something so terrible that I've buried it deep within myself, hidden even from my own consciousness?"

Sadie's eyes narrowed in thought. "Juliette, whatever it is, you don't face it alone."

Carenza nodded in agreement. "You're not defined by your past. Your actions now, your choices today and every day going forward, determine who you are."

Holding on to that, Juliette continued, recounting the ransacking of her modiste shop and the devastation wrought upon her flat. The brick through the shop window, the ominous messages—she shared it all.

Sadie's eyes blazed with fury. "Those damned Revivalists! To terrorize you in such a way, it's unforgivable!"

A sly smile curled Carenza's lips as a hard, fierce glint sparked in her blue eyes. "Well, I believe I have a plan," she announced. "Catamount and his Runners will be impressed."

Relief flooded Juliette.

She wasn't alone. She had Catamount, and his Bow Street Runners, and Sadie, and Carenza. She had people who cared.

"I knew coming to you for advice was the right course of action."

"Of course it was." Carenza beamed. "Cat's not the only one who in this family who can catch a criminal."

"Tell me your plan."

"Well, it begins with using you as bait."

CHAPTER EIGHTEEN

THE FLICKERING LAMPLIGHTS cast a golden glow on the cobbled streets as Catamount ascended the stairs to his flat. The weariness of a hard day as the captain of the Bow Street Runners weighed heavily on him. He and his men had searched all day for the murdering bastards with no luck.

His grumbling words resonated through the narrow corridor as he strode down it, a solitary rumble of discontent. "Bloody Revivalists. Slippery as eels, the lot of 'em. Can't make a damn move without them slithering away into the shadows."

As he reached the door to the flat, a peculiar sensation tugged at his heart. The rhythmic thumping in his chest intensified, a primal recognition that something awaited him beyond that familiar threshold. *Juliette.* Christ, he'd thought of her all day. *Felt* her all day, right in the center of his chest around his heart.

With a deliberate pause, he stood before the door, key in hand, the weight of the day gradually lifting as his mind danced on the edge of a revelation. The idea crept into his consciousness, unfurling like the tendrils of ivy on a brick wall—a realization that stirred feelings long veiled by the practicalities of his profession.

Having someone—*her*—to come home to was heavenly.

Taking a deep breath, he inserted the key into the lock, turning the mechanism with a quiet click. The door creaked open, and the faint light within spilled into the corridor, revealing the familiar contours of his flat. Pushing the door wide, he entered the room, scanning the space, expecting her to be there.

But she wasn't. Juliette wasn't there. His flat was empty.

The door swung shut behind him with a soft thud. A wave of panic seized Catamount as he swept his eyes across the familiar surroundings. It was as he feared all day—Juliette had left.

He barked into the room, "Juliette!" The name echoed, unanswered. A disquiet settled over him as he searched for any sign of her presence.

Then, in the stillness of the room, his attention was drawn to a small figure by the window. Her kitten, Odette, sat there, eyes wide and watchful.

"Where is she?" he demanded, his voice sharp and urgent. The kitten remained unmoved, a silent sentinel in the room that held the secrets of Juliette's absence. Nothing seemed amiss, and yet the air was charged with tension. "Where the hell did she go?"

A swell of emotion, something dangerously close to love, surged within Catamount's chest as he stood in the middle of his room. The fear that something might have befallen her stirred with the sentiment that he was hesitant to acknowledge. His mind, often clear and decisive, was clouded with emotions. The room pulsed with the imprint of her presence, each corner whispering the silent connection that had unexpectedly woven its threads into the fabric of his life.

He spotted a note on the table and clenched his jaw, impatient and frustrated. "Damn it, Juliette!" He snatched up the note, scanning her handwritten words. The note detailed her destination—a decision she'd made in defiance of his explicit instructions for her to stay put. The tension in the room heightened, responsibility he felt for her mingling with an undercurrent of something more profound—a sense of protectiveness tinged with a realization that Juliette's choices, however well intentioned, had the power to unravel the carefully constructed boundaries he had placed around her safety.

Catamount's frustration spilled out in gruff mutterings as he reread the note. "I told her to stay put, damn it. Can't she follow a simple order?" The kitten, perched nearby, observed as he paced, his agitation palpable. "Stubborn woman. Doesn't she understand the danger she's in? I can't protect her if she goes off on her own."

He turned toward the kitten, exasperated. "You'd think she'd listen, wouldn't you?"

The feline offered no response, merely blinked nonchalantly. Of course.

Catamount's frustration simmered beneath the surface as he grabbed his long coat. "Can't believe she went off on her own," he growled, his steps purposeful as he stormed out of his flat.

His expression was stern and his strides agitated as he navigated the familiar paths that led to Tipton House, his childhood home. "I've all my available men scouring the streets for the Revivalists, and she's off visiting my sisters like it's nothing. What the bloody hell?"

The evening air hung with a crisp bite, a reminder that autumn was giving way to the colder days of winter. The sun, having dipped below the horizon, left behind hues of twilight that painted the sky in soft shades of orange and pink. A gentle breeze carried the scent of fallen leaves, earthy and rich, through the quiet streets. Occasionally, the distant sounds of horse-drawn carriages added a rhythmic backdrop.

Overhead, the skeletal branches of trees stood stark against the fading light, their silhouettes etched against the darkening sky. November evenings held a certain melancholic beauty, a quiet transition between the vibrancy of autumn and the stillness of winter, a time when the world seemed to draw itself into a den of contemplation.

Consumed by frustration and worry, Catamount marched with a singular determination that left him oblivious to the encroaching chill, his mind preoccupied with thoughts of Juliette and the dangerous path she might have ventured onto.

The flickering gas lamps cast elongated shadows as he moved through the dimming streets, his long coat billowing behind him. His furrowed brow and clenched jaw betrayed his emotions, and people gave him a wide berth as he passed. Which was fine with him. More than fine.

Unless one of them was a Revivalist. Then he wanted to punch his face in. And more. Christ, he wanted to do so much more to them for hurting his Julie.

The weight of his frustration heavy upon him, Catamount stormed into the drawing room of Tipton House, expecting to find Juliette alone with his sister-in-law, Sadie. To his surprise, the room was filled with the entirety of his family. His mother, Crawford, Carenza's husband Damon, his sister Nora and her husband Rainville, his youngest sister Lottie and her brand-new husband Thatcher—all were gathered, creating an unexpected family gathering.

Fuck.

He stopped dead in his tracks. "What in blazes is going on here?" he demanded, the frustration that had fueled his journey finding a new target.

His mother, a picture of calmness, offered a smile that belied the underlying hurt. "Just a family dinner night, my son. You were, as always, invited. But, as always, you never replied."

Caught off guard by his mother's reproachful words, Catamount felt a twinge of guilt beneath the veneer of his frustration. The burden of responsibility, both to his family and to Juliette, weighed heavily on his shoulders.

He caught sight of the woman he sought right before she spoke. Juliette, obviously sensing the tense undercurrent, interjected in a diplomatic tone, "Your family has been gracious in inviting me to dinner. I appreciate the generosity of their welcome."

Like she hadn't left his home when she said she wouldn't, risking her life.

Her *life.*

How could she be so foolish with something so precious?

Catamount's eyes met Juliette's across the expansive drawing room, a promise hot in them—one that said very clearly that they would discuss her choices later. Her serene smile in response hinted at defiance.

His family laughed and chatted on around him, drawing Juliette into their animated discussion, and his attention drifted to the weight of the ring tucked safely in his inside coat pocket. His constant companion for three long years, it suddenly felt like a substantial burden—a tangible reminder of a life he'd already lost once. The heft of it lingered in his awareness, a symbol of promises yet to be fulfilled.

As his gaze lingered on Juliette, his mind drifted to the time when he had planned to propose to Julie. A surge of poignant emotions swelled within him—regret, sorrow, and the awful what-ifs of a love that never had the chance to fully bloom. The intensity of his feelings, not quite love but undeniably profound and close to it, welled up in his chest.

Crawford, ever perceptive, approached him. A knowing look passed over his face, and he spoke with a touch of playful teasing. "I see the way you're looking at her, Cat. Don't try to hide it," he remarked. In an instant Catamount's feelings were laid bare, acknowledged by a damnably perceptive brother. Leaning in close, Crawford whispered conspiratorially, "I can't help but notice how much Juliette resembles your beloved Julie." His pale blue eyes practically glittered with sympathy and curiosity.

"It's not the same," Catamount growled, a defensive edge in his voice.

His brother gave a small nod. "I know it's not the same, but the heart yearns for familiarity, even when the circumstances differ. Cat, brother," he said, studying Catamount's undoubtedly troubled expression, "I have to ask the hard but obvious question. Do you want Juliette for who she is, or are you hoping she'll fill a void left by Julie?"

Catamount scowled, caught off guard by the directness of the question. "I... I don't know, Craw. I just can't help but see Julie in her. And she's got memories of the Seven Dials attacks. Not of me and our time together, but of the Revivalist attack. Which places her there that night. You tell me that you wouldn't draw the same conclusion."

Crawford nodded sagely. "I hear you, Cat, I do. But the truth is that Juliette deserves to be loved and wanted for who *she* is, not as a replacement for someone else. Or because you *think* she might be someone else. Take your time, figure out your feelings for *her*—and for Christ's sake, be fair to her. You both deserve that."

Blast it, his brother was right. The heart's journey was complex.

Yet love, in its truest form, required only acceptance. For what was, not for what might be.

CHAPTER NINETEEN

THE LIBRARY AT Tipton House was refined elegance, its walls lined with rich mahogany shelves and volumes of tales from eras long past. The amber glow of a fireplace bathed the room in a soft radiance, casting shadows that danced across the rows of leather-bound books. A beautiful, peaceful place to spend the evening, Juliette decided as she followed behind Catamount, touring the room. Revivalists who?

Still draped in her day dress of delicate rose, she felt the crisp silk brush against her skin as he suddenly drew her close. "Catamount!" she squeaked in surprise. She squeaked again— breathlessly this time—when he grabbed a strand of her hair and rubbed it slowly between his fingers. Flooded with anticipation and desire, she met Catamount's gaze. The fragrance of aged paper, polished wood, and a hint of lavender permeated the air around them, and she breathed in deep.

As Catamount's golden-bronze hair caught the light, he leaned in, his voice a soft whisper against her ear. "You are an exquisite vision in that dress."

A playful smile graced her lips as she replied, "And you, dear captain, look impossibly handsome in pretty much anything. Though I must say, catching criminals suits you far less than moments like these."

Catamount chuckled. "Maybe I should spend more time in the library, then." His fingers traced a gentle path along the curve of her waist.

Their lips met in a lingering kiss, a delicate dance of passion, as Catamount guided her toward a plush settee, his hands on her waist. Juliette started to back up, but her foot caught on the edge of an ornate rug, sending them tumbling to the ground. A harsh thud echoed in the room, punctuating their descent.

The impact was harder than expected. She went down with a force that jolted her entire body, and her head connected abruptly with the unforgiving hardwood floor. The world spun for a moment, stars dancing in her vision as she fought the disorienting sensation that threatened to pull her into unconsciousness.

Concern etched Catamount's features as he rolled quickly off and knelt beside her. "Are you all right?" he asked, reaching out to gently cradle her face.

"The perils of grand romance," Juliette managed to quip, her eyes watering against the discomfort.

His concern deepened at the sight of her unshed tears, and he helped her sit up. "Are you certain you're all right?"

"I'm fine, truly," Juliette insisted, offering a reassuring smile while attempting to shake off the lingering dizziness. She tried to maintain a façade of composure, but the throbbing ache in her head and an unsettling queasiness in her stomach betrayed her efforts.

Catamount wasn't easily convinced. Blasted Bow Street instincts of his kicking in. "You took quite a spill. Let me get you some water or something."

The room swayed slightly as she nodded, grateful for his attentiveness. As Catamount hurried off to fetch water, she pressed a hand to her forehead, hoping the discomfort would pass soon.

When he returned with a glass of water, he crouched beside her. "Here, take it slow," he said, handing her the glass.

Juliette accepted the water gratefully, sipping it cautiously. The cool liquid provided a momentary respite, and she let out a soft sigh. Catamount's eyes never left her, his worry etched in the lines of his furrowed brow.

"Are you sure you're all right?" he asked a third time.

She nodded, managing a faint smile. "Just a bit shaken, I suppose. It's nothing serious."

He reached out, brushing a strand of hair from her face. "Maybe we should take a break from the acrobatics for now." Despite the circumstances, a playful glint sparked in his eyes.

"Perhaps you're right," she replied. "We wouldn't want any more unplanned tumbles."

Catamount grinned, worry easing from his expression. "No, we wouldn't. Let me help you up."

She took his hand. "I'm fine, really. You should head back to your family."

As he assisted her to her feet, their eyes met, something passing between them. "Are you certain, Juliette? I don't feel right leaving you alone if you're not feeling well."

She managed a reassuring smile, attempting to downplay her unease. "Truly, I just need a moment to compose myself. Go, enjoy their company. I'll catch up with you shortly."

Despite her words, he remained unconvinced. "If you need anything, don't hesitate to call. I'll be right in the drawing room with everyone."

"Thank you, I'll be fine. Now go." She shooed him away with a bright smile.

As he reluctantly left the room, Juliette dropped the smile and sank onto the settee, her hand pressed against her forehead. The pain from the fall lingered, but it was the unsettling feeling of elusive memories rising from her subconscious that troubled her the most. Flashes of a night she couldn't quite grasp taunted her, and she shivered involuntarily. Oh, how she wished there was a way to control when and how the visions came!

"Come on, Juliette," she whispered to herself, attempting to push away the encroaching shadows, acutely aware of the scene she might make if they overtook her. "You can handle this."

Yet uncertainty gnawed at her. She wondered what lay hidden in the recesses of her mind, waiting to be unearthed. As Juliette tried to collect herself, she couldn't shake the throbbing pain in her head. The fall seemed trivial in retrospect and not very injurious. Yet her temples pulsed with a ferocity that puzzled her. She closed her eyes, attempting to focus on the rhythmic inhale and exhale of her breath, hoping the discomfort would subside.

The firelight of the library fireplace danced through her closed eyelids, casting a warm glow on the inside of her consciousness. Still, the ache persisted. She massaged her temples in a futile attempt to alleviate the pain, questioning why such a minor incident could leave her feeling so disoriented.

In the hazy aftermath of the fall, whispers of forgotten memories flickered at the edges of her mind, elusive and fragmentary. She tried to dismiss them, attributing the disquiet to the physical aftermath of her tumble, but a lingering unease settled in the pit of her stomach.

Just then, Juliette's body seemed to lose its strength, and she practically sagged into the seat, overcome by a flood of memories. The library, with its richly adorned shelves and ornate furniture, blurred and turned into the tavern she once knew in Seven Dials. The vivid recollection of that dreadful night filled her mind with horrible images.

"They came in masks, like demons unleashed," she whispered to herself, her voice choked with fear. "The terror in their eyes, the brutality…" A shudder ran through her as the recollections carved a painful path through her consciousness.

The Revivalists.

The awful sound of screams and breaking glass in her mind intertwined with her very real sobs. She clutched her head, as if trying to ward off the memories that clawed at the edges of her mind. The pain in her head wasn't just from the fall; it was the resurgence of trauma, vivid and unrelenting.

Lost in her distress, Juliette whispered fragments of conversations she had had with herself that fateful night. As the pain in her head reached a blinding crescendo, a torrent of memories rushed back. The polished shelves of the library became a grim reminder of the rough-hewn bar she had cowered behind during the attack.

Screams of innocent patrons, their lives cut short by the merciless Revivalists, rang in her mind. Her heart pounded as the nightmare scenes unfolded before her eyes. She saw it. Felt it. *Relived* it.

She was back there once more, hiding behind the bar, watching in horror as the Revivalists callously took lives. They fell, those poor people, one after the other. Nothing but blood everywhere.

Amidst the resurgence of haunting memories, Juliette's breath hitched, and her voice shook as she whispered to herself, "No… no. I can't relive that night."

But she *did*.

Terror reverberated through her as she recalled the desperate pleas of the innocent patrons. "Hide, Juliette! Hide!" a voice cried out in her memory.

As the visions intensified even more, she could feel the cold sweat on her palms, recalled the metallic tang of fear in the air. Her heartbeat thudded in her ears, synchronizing with the anguished cries of the wounded.

And suddenly there was a Revivalist, bleeding and dying, lying near her on the tavern floor, his gaze locked accusingly on her. And in an instant, Juliette knew the truth. The whole truth. The awful, horrible truth that her mind had tried to bury and forget. She wasn't innocent. Not even remotely.

"Oh God," she cried out. "I took his money, and I lied for them…" she sobbed, the weight of guilt settling heavily on her conscience.

Choices have consequences, a spectral voice seemed to murmur, and Juliette's eyes filled with tears as the library walls closed in, witness to her painful revelation.

The air in the room thickened as Juliette was plunged into the harrowing memories. The wounded Revivalist beside her was stirring, gasping for breath. His bloodstained hand reached out, and he managed a weak plea: "Help me…"

The bag of money he'd given to her, clutched against her chest, felt heavy, a cruel reminder of the choices she had made. "Stay quiet," she whispered to herself, her voice shaky. She hesitated, torn between compassion and self-preservation.

The wounded Revivalist's eyes met hers, a desperate plea for mercy. "Please… don't let me die here."

"I can't help you," she muttered, her hands trembling as she clung to the ill-gotten gains. The tavern shadows whispered accusations, and Juliette, torn by guilt, felt the room closing in on her.

Survive, a voice echoed in her mind, urging her to make a choice as that fateful night finally unfolded in her mind with painful clarity.

The man's eyes, filled with rage and fixated on Juliette and the money clutched in her hands. His labored breaths turning into menacing growls as he struggled to sit up. In the dim tavern, death danced grotesquely around them. "You thieving wench!" he spat. The darkness of the room seemed to amplify the malice in his words. "I had a deal with you," he seethed, clutching his wounded abdomen. "You were supposed to ensure our escape, not rob me blind."

Juliette's mind raced as fear and regret twisted within her. She had underestimated the ruthlessness of the man she had made a deal with.

Survive, the haunting voice whispered again, this time a cruel reminder of the compromises she had made.

She held the bag to her chest and ran.

The alley was as far as she made it before he caught up to her, staggering toward Juliette. "You won't get away with this," he snarled, a twisted grin revealing bloodstained teeth. "You stole from us, and now you'll pay."

Juliette's heart pounded as she stumbled backward, clutching the money bag. The alley seemed to close in around her, and the Revivalist lunged at her.

As his first blow landed, the memories flooded back to her like a violent storm. The sharp pain, the metallic taste of blood, and the desperate struggle for survival played out in a cruel dance. "I paid you!" he spat between blows, the weight of each word landing like his physical assault. The money bag slipped from her grasp, scattering gold coins like a bitter rain.

The room spun as Juliette's mind recoiled from the vivid images. She winced at the memory of the cold alley floor against her back, the sting of each fist strike, and the desperate gasps for breath. A surge of nausea clawed at her as she relived the moment when her assailant's grip tightened around her throat. "You thought you could escape with our money, didn't you? No one betrays the Revivalists."

In the library, she shuddered, grappling with the visceral memories.

As the Revivalist's grip tightened, her world narrowed to a suffocating point. And then, with a primal instinct for survival, Juliette fought back. The sharp glint of a pair of fabric scissors gleamed in her hand as she yanked them from the pocket of her skirts and slashed at her assailant.

Back in the library, Juliette clutched the arms of the chair. She grappled with the haunting truth that had finally clawed its way to the surface. She grappled with the torrent of memories, and the sensation of being dragged across the cold cobblestones lingered.

And then, abruptly, everything went black.

The abruptness of the memory's end left her suspended in a void, the aftermath of violence and trauma echoing through the recesses of her consciousness. Tears streamed down her face as her suppressed memories bore down on her. Sobs escaped from deep within, carrying the shame and guilt of that night in Seven Dials.

The taste of copper lingered in the back of her throat, a cruel reminder of the blood spilled that night—blood she had touched, blood she had failed to prevent from staining her hands. She had taken that money. She had been a part of it all.

Juliette felt the sting of shame, an unrelenting force that threatened to consume her.

Each sob carried self-reproach, a poignant soundtrack to the revelation of her own complicity in the darkness that had shadowed her past. Her voice, barely audible between sobs, wavered as she whispered to herself, "I took their money… The bag of coins. What have I done?" As she clutched the chair, the memory of the Revivalist's anger fueled her self-recrimination. "He was a killer, a monster," she muttered, as if attempting to rationalize her actions to the empty room. Like stealing wasn't stealing. Theft not theft.

Words kept tumbling out in disjointed fragments. "I betrayed my beliefs… and for what? Money?"

The library's stillness offered no judgment, only the soft creaking of floorboards beneath her feet.

"I thought with that money that I was escaping the hardships of London with Catamount. A fresh start, a chance for happiness," she confessed. "But I became a pawn in their game," she continued, her voice choked with despair. "A puppet, dancing to their malevolent tune. I… I lied to Catamount for them, betrayed the one person who cared for me. I let them use me. I let myself become a part of their awfulness. It doesn't matter that I knew not who the nobleman was when I agreed to tell Catamount the information he gave me. All I saw was a chance for a better life for me, for *us*, and I took it—even when my conscience told me not to."

In the flickering candlelight, surrounded by the whispers of the past, Juliette grappled with the darkness within herself. "I knew it was wrong, telling Catamount I overheard talk of the Revivalists attacking in Lambeth. I sent the Runners on a wild goose chase while people died. Damn me!"

She pushed herself up from the seat. "I can't stay here. I don't deserve him, his love, or the life we could have," she whispered to herself. The library now felt like a prison of her own making.

With hurried steps, Juliette crossed the room, her mind racing with the urgency to set things right. The grandeur of Tipton House faded into insignificance against the riot in her heart. "I have to leave," she murmured, brushing her fingers over the ornate doorknob. The door creaked open, a portal to a path she believed she must tread alone. As punishment for her past deeds.

Her breaths came quick. "I'll find a way to make amends, to fix what I've broken," she vowed. "I can't bring those people back, but I can do something right for once." With a final glance back at the library, she stepped into the corridor, her past mistakes driving her toward a daunting journey of redemption. Finding a servant, she sent Catamount the message that her head ached, and she was going to lie down in one of the guest rooms, perhaps for the rest of the night. It would be best if he went home and did not wait for her. With the message sent, she slipped silently upstairs to Carenza's bedchamber.

The pale glow of moonlight spilled through the lace curtains of the viscountess's room as Juliette tiptoed across the plush carpet. Her heartbeat thundered in her ears, a nervous symphony accompanying the gravity of her decision. Carenza's room was familiar from the times she had done an alteration or fitting there, yet Juliette felt like an intruder in her friend's private sanctuary.

With careful steps, she approached the window, its heavy curtains drawn slightly apart. A gentle breeze stirred the room, carrying a scent of roses from the gardens below. The small terrace beckoned like a secret escape, and Juliette's trembling fingers worked to open the window wider. As she stepped onto the tiny terrace, the cool night air brushed against her cheeks. The moonlit world beyond Tipton House unfolded, a place of shadows and secrets. The scent of night-blooming flowers filled the air, mingling with the distant sounds of carriage wheels and hushed whispers of the night.

Juliette took a deep breath, her past pressing upon her. Memories of the Revivalists and the choices she had made clawed at the edges of her consciousness. She hesitated for a moment, torn between the safety of the life she had known for the past three years and the daunting journey that awaited her beyond the ivy-covered tree.

Summoning the courage to face her own mistakes, Juliette began her descent down the tree. The moon cast elongated shadows across the garden. The ivy leaves rustled beneath her fingertips—a whispering chorus of encouragement or warning, she couldn't tell.

When her feet finally touched the ground, the city of London stretched before her. Juliette squared her shoulders, determined to forge a new destiny.

"I took their money, lied to Catamount, and became a part of their wicked plan," she murmured to herself, the words carried away by the night breeze as she shimmied down the tree. "It's my mess, and I have to clean it up."

On a mission, Juliette slipped away into the inky night of London.

CHAPTER TWENTY

CATAMOUNT'S EYES SNAPPED open to the emptiness beside him. He bolted out of bed, his senses immediately alert. He scanned the room, finding no remnants of another presence—no indentation on the pillow next to him, or the faint scent of Juliette's hair lingering in the air.

"Juliette?" he called out, the room echoing with the sharpness of his voice. Panic gripped him as he searched every corner of his flat, his steps quick and purposeful. The kitten, startled by the sudden commotion, darted across his path, causing Catamount to stumble. "Cursed furball," he muttered. He continued his search, calling out her name at intervals, the silence that followed each call amplifying the growing unease within him. "The maid said she'd probably stay the night. I shouldn't panic."

He stopped abruptly, his eyes narrowing as he scanned the room for any clues. There was no note, no explanation for her continued absence. His unease deepened, twisting into a knot of worry that tightened with each passing moment.

Catamount's mind raced, considering the possibilities. Then his broad shoulders slumped, and he found himself muttering aloud, a raw vulnerability in his usually steady voice. Bare-chested, he moved through the room, his barefoot steps slapping against the wood floors. "Where are you, Juliette?"

The room, bathed in the soft glow of early morning light, seemed to amplify the silence that surrounded him. Catamount's eyes darted from corner to corner, searching for a trace of her, as if he were willing Juliette to reappear before him.

A creak in the floorboards drew his attention, and he turned abruptly, half expecting to find Juliette standing there, a teasing smile on her lips. But the room remained empty, and the reality of her absence settled in. "Damn it, Juliette," he said. The ache in his chest tightened, and he sank onto the edge of the bed. "Why are you always disappearing?" One would think an experienced Runner would be better at keeping track of someone.

Odette, sensing his distress, padded over and nudged his leg. Catamount absent-mindedly stroked her fur, his mind still racing through the possibilities. Where could Juliette have gone? What danger might she be facing? Christ, did the Revivalists get to her?

"No, you fool. She's just resting at Tipton House. Stop imagining the worst."

The sudden pounding on the front door reverberated through the room. Catamount swore and moved swiftly, swinging the door open to reveal one of his Runners, a young man with a disheveled appearance, panting and wide-eyed. "Captain, you've got to hear this!" the Runner blurted out, his words tumbling over each other in his excitement.

Catamount's instincts went on high alert. "What is it, Simmons? Speak quickly. I think Juliette's missing."

Simmons took a moment to catch his breath before launching into his report. "Word's spread like wildfire, sir. The Revivalists have been spotted near Bond Street. They're up to something, and the whole headquarters is buzzing with it." They'd never ventured outside the rookeries and Docklands before. This was new.

"What exactly did the sources say?"

Simmons stammered for a moment before regaining his composure. "There've been whispers of a gathering, sir. Some say they're planning a retaliation for the recent investigations."

Dread crept over Catamount at the Revivalists being spotted near Bond Street. A cold fear gripped his heart, and he grabbed the young Runner's sleeve, his mind belatedly connecting the dots. "Bond Street," he muttered, realization hitting him like a blow. "Juliette's shop is on Bond Street, and she wanted to go there despite my warnings. Shite, I bet that's where she is now." Catamount's sense of urgency intensified, and he barked orders to his man. "We're heading to Bond Street. Now!" The urgency in his voice spurred the Runner into immediate action, and Simmons moved with purpose.

Catamount's mind raced with worry for Juliette. He cursed himself under his breath as he hastily threw on his clothes. "Should've stuck by her side. Bloody fool," he muttered.

Cold dread ran down his spine as he imagined Juliette alone in her shop, unaware of the looming danger. The Revivalists were a threat he couldn't underestimate, especially when it came to someone he held dear. He rushed to gather his belongings and head to Bond Street.

Just when he was about to leave, the door to his flat swung open, and in burst Carenza and Sadie, a whirlwind of skirts and noise. Their presence filled the room with a swirl of energy.

"Catamount, she's baiting the Revivalists into a trap!" Carenza's eyes blazed with concern.

Catamount's heart roared within him, a cacophony of love and fear colliding. The conflicting emotions manifested in a guttural growl as he cursed under his breath. "She's what?"

Sadie stepped forward. "She believes she can draw them out, catch them in the act. It's risky, but she's determined to end this and believes she can."

"Is she insane? Dammit, Juliette," he muttered.

Carenza laid a hand on his arm. "We need to help her, Catamount. She's not alone. We're all in this together."

"Of course we are." He looked at Sadie and Carenza, torn between his instinct to protect and the reality of Juliette's courage. With fierce resolve, he nodded. "Let's move. We don't have time to waste."

CHAPTER TWENTY-ONE

T HEY WERE WATCHING her.

Every hair on the back of her neck rose as the sensation swept over her, alerting her and sending alarm ringing through her mind. "Finally," she muttered. How long had she been strolling along Piccadilly and Bond Streets with the bag from Seven Dials, trying to gain the Revivalists' attention like a doxy seeking customers? Hours, perhaps? Long enough for her to intimately understand the way a peacock must feel when showing off to attract attention—a bit foolish and decidedly cheap.

But it worked.

Eyes bored into her back, sharp as a thousand daggers, weeping of ill intent.

Remember, directly up to your flat to draw them into one single, contained space for Catamount and his Runners to seize them. Though she wanted to glance over her shoulder and break into a dead run, she held her pace steady. *Only a few more steps.*

Her shop came into view, and her hands shook terribly as she opened the door and rushed through. The familiar sights and scents instantly comforted her nerves, though it was short-lived. "Upstairs," she panted, thankful Odette remained safe and protected at Catamount's home.

Catamount.

As she ran through the shop toward the back stairs leading to her flat, her mind flashed to the very first time she met him, the memory clear and strong. Blessedly, beautifully clear, after three confusing, heart-aching years of fog. He been the most captivating man she'd ever seen.

"Whisky, please," he'd said, sliding onto a stool at the tavern she worked at in the hub of Seven Dials, his voice weary and rough and so incredibly masculine. Like him. Every inch of him had been rugged and tough. Even his eyes, crystalline green, held a world-weariness in them that had not just tugged at her heart, but yanked it right out of her chest to land right in his hands.

"What's your name?" she'd asked, her stomach quivering at this bronze-haired man in a long, dusty coat.

"Catamount," he grunted, and swiped a hand across his unshaven jaw and up through his hair, tousling the blond-tipped strands. "Yours?"

"Julie, *monsieur*." She rounded the long bar and began pouring him a drink when she spotted no sight of the owner who normally manned the taps and bar. "Catamount... That's an unusual name, no? What does it mean?"

"It means 'big cat.'" His eyes slid across the bar top to her, the intensity of them boring through her, like a predator sighting prey.

The name made sense.

"My mother insisted," he added, his deep voice resonating in the pit of her belly. His gaze flicked over her from her auburn curls struggling against the confines of their pins, down to her worn work boots, and back up to rest briefly on her freckles before meeting hers. "While carrying me, my father read letters her cousin sent from America, detailing the creatures he encountered as he explored the vast land, and he often wrote about these enormous, powerful cats the Americans called catamounts. She thought by naming me that, I'd be equally as strong and powerful." He smirked and took a sip of the drink she'd placed before him. "Not sure why I just told you that."

"I have that look about me," she said around a smile, liking this man very much. "What do you do, Monsieur Catamount?

"I'm with the Bow Street Runners. Captain Catamount Castlebury at your service."

She laughed then, the sound ringing out across the dingy tavern, filled with delight. "Well, seems your mother was right."

Her mind whipped back to the present just in time.

Juliette hit the landing to her flat at a dead run, nearly ramming into her door in her haste to get inside. *"Merde,"* she grunted, fumbling with the doorknob.

The door downstairs crashed open, the sound of splintering wood echoing through the shop.

The Revivalists had arrived.

"Merde!" she swore again. Shaking violently, she fought the door open and crumpled against it once she was inside. "Hurry, Catamount," she pleaded under her breath, clutching the empty carpetbag to her chest. "Please hurry."

Suddenly the door behind her trembled, fists pounding hard and angry against the barrier. "We know you're in there!" one of them called, his voice sickening in its glee.

Taking a deep breath, Juliette reached down deep for the survivor in her—that tough and capable part that had seen her through a life fraught with hardships—and pushed away from the door.

It was time to face her tormentors.

The air in her flat hung heavy with tension as the six ominous figures of the Revivalists splintered her front door, shattering it to pieces, and closed in around her. Each of them, a nobleman draped in black clothes, exuded danger that sent shivers down her spine. But she refused to show cowardice.

"You'll rue the day you crossed me," she warned on a bluff. "I've the Bow Street Runners on my side." At the front of the group of murdering madmen was the one she recognized, the man she had made a deal with on that fateful night in Seven Dials three years ago. His eyes, dark and penetrating, held a burning anger that seemed to sear into her soul. "I thought you were dead!" she exclaimed.

"Only in your dreams, poppet. I survived and I want my money back. That was an awful lot you stole, you know."

"I-I don't have it!" Juliette shook her head. "I promise." She'd spent it all on buying her shop and the things within it. The money itself was long gone.

"You thought you could escape us," he sneered, a malicious grin twisting his features. "That we wouldn't find you."

To his left, a tall and imposing figure stood with a cold, calculating demeanor. His gaze, sharp as a blade, assessed Juliette with a detached cruelty that set her on edge. "You couldn't hide forever," he declared.

A man with a pox-scarred face approached. Even though he wore a mask, she instantly recognized him as Lord Breyer, a daily patron of the tobacconist directly across from her shop. "You played a dangerous, losing game, my lady," he remarked, his tone laced with a dark amusement.

Behind them, a pair of identical twins moved with an eerie synchronicity. The Turlington brothers. The "elder" twin was heir to an ancient viscountcy. She knew because she dressed their mother, Lady Agnes, and she gossiped something fierce. "We've been watching you," one of them whispered, the words sending a chill down Juliette's spine.

Completing the sinister ensemble was a man with a lean, predatory grace. His movements were calculated, and his eyes gleamed with an unsettling hunger. "It's time to pay for your sins," he hissed.

Juliette knew that if she were more knowledgeable of the peerage, she would be able to identify them all.

The memories of that night in Seven Dials flooded back again, her past choices standing before her, ready for revenge.

The one with whom Juliette had made that ill-fated deal stepped forward with a sinister grin. "You thought you could align yourself with the captain of the Bow Street Runners and betray us without consequences? Like we wouldn't know what you were up to."

Juliette, her back against the wall, squared her shoulders. "I'm not your pawn anymore. I won't be manipulated by the likes of you."

The scarred man chuckled darkly. "You're playing a dangerous game, modiste. Crossing paths with a Runner won't save you."

With a mocking smile, the tall figure added, "You might have escaped us once, but your little alliance won't shield you forever."

The twins echoed in eerie unison, "We know what you did, Juliette. You can't erase the past."

One of them hissed, "Catamount Castlebury won't protect you. He can't."

Juliette, her voice steady despite the rising terror, shot back, "Catamount is more than you think. And he will protect me." In fact, he should be storming the door to the shop below any moment now.

She was relying on it.

Relying on *him*.

The leader's eyes flared with anger. "You've sealed your fate, barmaid. This is the end of the line for you." He circled her. "You took our money and betrayed your precious Bow Street Runner. You're no different from us. Just a player in this sordid game."

"I did what I had to survive that night. But I won't let you continue your reign of terror. Yes, I took your money! You bloody paid it to me to tell him about the attack, and I did." And people had died because of it. She had to live with that knowledge every day for the rest of her life.

The scarred man scoffed, "Survival is often a matter of perspective. You enjoyed the spoils of our actions, all while pretending to be the innocent, forgetful victim."

The twins chimed in, their voices a disconcerting harmony, "You're a traitor, Juliette. A deceiver. Catamount Castlebury will know the truth about you."

Lord Breyer spoke, his gaze piercing through the shadows. "Your love for the Runner won't save you from the consequences of your bad choices."

Juliette, defiance burning within her, retorted, "I'll face the consequences, but I won't let you destroy the lives of innocent people any longer. I took that money to escape this wretched city, to create a life far from the darkness you bring. A life with Catamount, free from your terror."

The leader sneered, "A life of luxury funded by the suffering of others. You're no different. Just a selfish whore in our twisted game."

She shook her head. "I'll never be like you. I've fought to build a different life, one filled with love and goodness. One that helps people, not hurts them."

Laughter echoed in the small living room. "Love, dear Juliette? Love won't erase the choices you made."

Lord Breyer stepped closer. "Your fate is tied to ours."

"I choose love over darkness, and I'll fight for it until my last breath," Juliette returned.

The leader seized her arm in a bruising grip. "I'm going to enjoy your agony," he said.

She winced at the pain but refused to let fear dominate her spirit. "If my fate is entwined with yours, then I'll face it on my terms, not yours." Juliette's mind raced, searching for a way to turn the tide.

That was when she heard it.

Her heart skipped a beat at the familiar birdcall, a secret song shared only between her and Catamount. A communication call they had set up long ago, from when she was Julie. Hope surged within her as she gathered her strength, ready to face whatever unfolded.

The leader sneered, oblivious to the significance of the sound. "Your lover won't save you. No one will. You're all alone."

Juliette's focus remained on the window past his shoulder. "He'll find me, and you'll pay for every ounce of pain you've caused."

The leader's slap landed with a sharp crack, leaving Juliette momentarily stunned. Her cheek burned, but her defiant spark remained. As she steadied herself, she locked eyes with the Revivalist, whose sneer conveyed a twisted satisfaction at her pain. "Is this your way of proving loyalty, my dear Juliette?" he taunted her, circling like a vulture closing in on its prey. "I like your cries."

A cold wind whispered through the room then, carrying with it the distant sound of footsteps. Juliette's heart quickened as she recognized the rhythmic cadence of Catamount's approach. With every step, her anticipation built, but she couldn't let on that she'd heard him.

The leader, growing impatient, raised his hand for another strike. Juliette, however, stood firm. "I'll never be like you. I won't let you tarnish the life I've built," she declared.

"It's already tarnished. You paid for it with blood money." The room filled with the tense energy of impending violence. The sick smell of it nearly gagged her. "You think your precious captain will save you? He won't. Not this time."

"You don't know the man you're up against." As Catamount's secret call echoed outside, Juliette met the leader's gaze with a triumphant smile. "He knows exactly who I am, and he's still coming for me."

Her own whistle echoed through the desolation of her ransacked flat. The Revivalists sneered, seemingly unimpressed by her attempt to signal for help.

"You think anyone can save you from us?" the leader said, slapping her once more.

Juliette tasted blood but met his gaze with a furious glare, tightly clutching the concealed fabric scissors she'd used before. She knew she had only moments before Catamount arrived.

As the Revivalists closed in on her, she surreptitiously tightened her grip on the fabric scissors, her eyes darting from one assailant to another. Just as they closed in, another birdcall pierced through the oppressive air.

Catamount was just beyond the flat's front door.

The leader of the Revivalists scowled, sensing the shift in the atmosphere. "What's that blasted noise?"

"You'll soon find out," Juliette replied.

The room seemed to vibrate with tension as the seconds stretched, and then, with a resounding crash, the door burst open. Catamount stormed in, eyes ablaze with fury.

A squadron of Bow Street Runners flooded the room, each one armed and poised for battle. The Revivalists, caught off guard by the sudden onslaught, found themselves outnumbered and outgunned.

Catamount's voice cut through the tension like a blade. "Stand down, Revivalists! Your reign of terror ends here."

The room crackled with charged energy as the Runners fanned out, their weapons trained on the nefarious group. The Revivalist leader, now realizing the tables had turned, spat defiantly, "You can't stop us, Castlebury. This city belongs to us!"

Catamount's response was a steely glare, his hand poised near the hilt of his weapon. "You underestimate the resolve of Bow Street. Surrender peacefully, and maybe justice will be kinder than you deserve."

The confrontation escalated as the Revivalists, unwilling to surrender, lashed out with a sudden burst of violence. In the chaos that ensued, Catamount and the Bow Street Runners expertly navigated the onslaught, their training and resolve evident in every coordinated move.

During the struggle, Juliette, her grip firm on the fabric scissors, found herself face to face with the leader. His eyes, filled with a desperate fury, locked on to hers. "You think this changes anything, barmaid? London will burn, and we'll rise from the ashes."

"I think not," she replied, kneeing him in his bollocks with all her might.

With a howl of pain, he dropped to his knees and clutched his groin. Catamount swiftly intervened, disarming the leader and bringing an end to the resistance. The Revivalists, now defeated and subdued, glared defiantly, their dreams of a malevolent empire shattered.

With the threat at last neutralized, Catamount turned to Juliette. "Are you hurt, love?"

She shook her head, the adrenaline still coursing through her veins. "I'm fine."

The Runners efficiently secured the Revivalists. As they were led away, the room seemed to sigh in relief.

Juliette met Catamount's gaze. "We faced them together," she murmured. "Just like you said."

Catamount, his expression full of pride and relief, nodded. "London is safe now, thanks to you."

With the immediate threat quelled, the adrenaline that had fueled her dissolved into a flood of emotions. She stumbled back on a sob, and Catamount was there, his strong arms enveloping her in a protective embrace. Juliette's tears, long held back in the face of danger and uncertainty, flowed freely. The sobs racked her body as the reality of the ordeal, the memories of Seven Dials, and the recent confrontation overwhelmed her.

"It's over, Julie," he whispered, holding her close. "You're safe now."

But in the aftermath of the confrontation, Juliette couldn't escape the shadows of her past actions. The choices she'd made, the deals with the Revivalist leader, the lies told to herself and Catamount—it all surged to the surface. The warmth of Catamount's presence offered solace, yet the burden of her guilt lingered.

"I didn't want to lose you," she confessed through choked sobs. "But I betrayed you. I took their money, and I lied."

Catamount, though undoubtedly grappling with his own complex emotions, remained a steadfast anchor. "Whatever happened, we'll find a way through."

Juliette was compelled to lay bare her truth, and steeled herself to reveal the tangled web of deceit she had woven. She needed to get it out.

"Catamount," she began, her voice trembling with remorse, "that night, when I took that money and lied to you about the Revivalists' plans, I... I didn't know. I didn't know who he was, what he represented. All I could see was an escape from my life of poverty, a chance to finally leave London with you." Her words hung in the air, the gravity of her admission settling between them. Catamount's expression remained steady, urging her to continue. "I thought it was a real tip, one that would afford us a chance to start anew. I didn't realize the danger, the darkness I was getting us into."

⇻⇻⇻⇺⇺⇺

THE REVELATION STRUCK Catamount like a physical blow, the realization of the depth of Juliette's actions hitting him with a force that threatened to knock the breath from his lungs. "You sent my men to the wrong place that night, jeopardizing lives," he said, each word clipped with a restrained fury. "And you did it on purpose?"

Juliette winced. "I didn't know... I-I didn't realize the consequences," she stammered. "I honestly thought I was giving a real tip, even though he paid me."

"Didn't the amount he gave you give you pause? Make you question it?"

She shook her head. "No, because he didn't give me much. Just a few coins. It wasn't until the attack when I thought he was dying that I saw the bag of money and took it."

The room felt charged with tension, the air heavy with truth laid bare. Catamount, who had dedicated his life to upholding justice, grappled with the harsh reality that the person he loved had played a role in the destruction that unfolded that night. "I trusted you with the safety of my men, with the safety of innocent lives," he bit out.

Juliette bowed her head, the consequences of her actions

settling heavily on her shoulders. The silence hung between them, a stark contrast to the chaos they had just emerged from. The connection they shared strained under the burden of her deception and betrayal.

"The lives lost that night, the families shattered…" He trailed off, unable to find the words to encapsulate the magnitude of the tragedy.

Juliette's eyes welled with tears. "I never meant for any of that to happen. I didn't understand what I was doing."

Catamount clenched his jaw, the conflicting emotions warring within him. He had seen the devastation firsthand, the aftermath of that merciless attack on Seven Dials. The faces of the victims haunted his dreams, and now he grappled with the realization that someone he loved had inadvertently played a role in the tragedy.

"I need time," he finally muttered, his voice strained. "I need time to understand this."

⫷⫸

JULIETTE NODDED AS Catamount turned away, his strides purposeful as he distanced himself from her. Each step resonated with the echoes of a love tarnished by betrayal and the shadows of a past that refused to loosen its grip.

Juliette stood there. The chasm that had opened between them seemed insurmountable. She reached out, a desperate plea in her eyes, but he continued his silent departure.

He paused, his back turned to her, as if wrestling with his own emotions. But then he sighed, opened the door, and strode through. She watched him go, her heart shattering.

Unexpectedly, he suddenly pivoted on his heel and marched back to her. His eyes locked on to hers. "I never cared about the money, Juliette. Not then, not now," he declared. "I wanted a life with you, just as you are. Poverty or wealth, it never mattered. It was always about us. About how much I loved you."

The sincerity in his words washed over Juliette, and a glimmer of hope flickered.

"I lost you that night, but I don't want to lose you again. We'll work this out together, as we always should have." He reached for her, gently cradling her face in his hands, wiping away the tears with his thumbs. "I love you, Juliette. Not the version of you I had in my head, not the Julie you were, but *you*. Flaws, mistakes, and all."

In that moment, a new foundation seemed to form. The barriers that had separated them began to crumble, leaving room for understanding and forgiveness. Love, resilient and enduring, emerged as the guiding force that could bind their wounded hearts together once more.

Catamount fumbled with something in the inner pocket of his coat and withdrew a small velvet box. The hinge softly creaked as he opened it, revealing a glimmering ring nestled within. He looked up at her with an intensity that matched the gleam of the ring. "Juliette Toussaint, will you marry me?" His voice wavered slightly, imbued with hope and vulnerability, and his eyes bored into hers with an unwavering sincerity.

Juliette's breath caught in her throat, and she blinked away tears. "Catamount, after everything…"

He silenced her with a gentle finger on her lips. "I don't care about the past, only the future. A future with you. I wanted to do this the night you died, and I never got the chance. I've been holding on to it ever since. So, will you be my wife, Juliette?"

He sank to one knee, holding the open box toward her, a symbol of hope and a promise for a future they could shape together. The room seemed to hold its breath as they stood on the precipice of a new beginning.

"Yes, a million times yes," she replied, throwing herself into his arms. "But call me Julie."

EPILOGUE

J ULIETTE REVELED IN the warmth of the summer day as she strolled through the sprawling gardens surrounding the country estate. The air was thick with the scent of blooming flowers, and the distant sounds of laughter and friendly arguments wafted toward her from the cricket pitch where her family engaged in a spirited game.

She cradled her gently rounding belly, feeling the reassuring flutter of life within. The vibrant hues of the garden seemed to mirror the joy she felt within her heart.

As she meandered along the gravel pathways, Juliette could hear the animated discussions and good-natured banter emanating from the gathering inside the manor house. The drawing room, filled with an assortment of Castlebury family members, rang with the clinking of teacups and laughter.

A breeze carried the sounds of cricket players bickering and playfully teasing each other as she continued her stroll. The verdant landscape spread before her, a patchwork of colors beneath the azure sky, as if celebrating the happiness that had taken root in the once-troubled soil of her past.

Juliette paused by a rose-covered arbor, taking in the delicate fragrance and smiling at the sight of children chasing butterflies as they sped past. The delicate folds of her summer dress swayed with the rhythm of her steps as she wandered through the estate's idyllic grounds. It still amazed her that she called this place home.

Catamount's rugged form emerged from behind a topiary as he made his way toward her with a grin that clearly showed the joy in his heart. "Juliette," he called. "The teams are getting rowdy over there. They need their captain to bring order."

She laughed, the sound carrying on the summer breeze. "I'll join them soon, my love. Our little one and I are enjoying the tranquility out here."

Catamount approached, his eyes softening as he placed a gentle hand on her growing bump. "Our family, our home—it's all thanks to you, Juliette. I love you."

The serenity of the estate, the laughter of family, and the promise of new life enveloped Juliette. As they headed back toward the spirited cricket gathering, she marveled at the journey that had led them to this moment, grateful every day for the love that had bloomed and flourished, just like the summer gardens surrounding their haven of happiness.

The vibrant chatter grew louder as Juliette and Catamount approached the lively scene. She felt a swell of gratitude for the newfound sense of belonging she had discovered with this family.

Nora, Catamount's younger sister, waved excitedly from a cluster of animated cousins and spouses, urging her to join the ongoing debate about the rules of the match. "We need you, Jules." Rainville, Damon, and even Lottie's husband Thatcher were passionately discussing strategies and team compositions, their enthusiasm infectious.

Catamount squeezed Juliette's hand, sharing a conspiratorial smile.

As they settled into the lively discussions and laughter, Juliette marveled at the intricacies of family dynamics—the inside jokes, shared glances, and unspoken understandings. Her heart swelled with appreciation for the connections that had mended the fractures of her past.

Amidst the laughter and camaraderie, Catamount leaned close to Juliette, his voice a soft murmur in her ear. "This is everything I ever wanted. A life filled with love, laughter, and a future with you."

She met his gaze, her heart agreeing completely with his sentiments. In that moment, surrounded by the love of the Castlebury family, Juliette embraced the beauty of her present and the promise of a future intertwined with the man she loved. "Let's go play some cricket, shall we?"

The expansive green fields stretched out before them, dotted with wildflowers and framed by ancient trees whose branches whispered tales of centuries past. The cricket pitch, a meticulously manicured patch of grass, became the stage for their family cricket match. The wickets stood tall, and the sound of leather against willow reverberated through the air as they all took turns batting and bowling. The jovial banter of family members mingled with the occasional thud of a well-hit cricket ball.

Juliette, her belly gently cradled by the soft fabric of her summer dress, laughed along with the others as she attempted to navigate the uneven terrain. Catamount, always the protective presence, hovered nearby, ready to catch her if needed. His booming laughter echoed across the field as he chided Thatcher for a particularly creative yet unsuccessful bowling attempt. "Goodrich, my man, I think you're aiming for the moon with that one! Stick to the basics," he teased, a twinkle in his pale green eyes.

Thatcher, undeterred, shot back with a grin, "Well, not all of us can be cricket legends. Some of us have to add a bit of artistic flair!"

The others joined in the friendly ribbing, each contributing their unique brand of humor. Juliette, now seated on a blanket near the sidelines, couldn't help but chuckle at the camaraderie.

Nora, wielding the cricket bat with confidence, exchanged playful jabs with Rainville. "My love, you bowl as if you're handling delicate china. Give it some power!"

Rainville feigned offense. "Delicate china, you say? I'll have you know my bowling has plenty of finesse!"

Soon Juliette's growing belly became a topic of affectionate ribbing.

Carenza, her sapphire-blue eyes sparkling, remarked, "My dear, I think you're carrying a future cricket champion in there!"

Juliette laughed along, enjoying the lively atmosphere. "Well, I'll make sure to teach them the art of a perfect cover drive from the very beginning."

Later, in the shade of the ancient oak tree, Catamount pulled Juliette close, cradling her round belly with tender reverence. The soft rustle of leaves overhead created a private cocoon, shielding them from the playful arguing of the ongoing match. His eyes, usually intense and guarded, softened with an unmistakable warmth as he gazed at her. "I love you," he murmured, the words carrying a depth of emotion that touched her soul.

A gentle breeze stirred Juliette's hair as she looked up at him. The world melted away as their lips met, a shared exchange of tenderness and devotion. The air around them buzzed with the timeless promise of love.

As the kiss deepened, a sense of completeness settled over Juliette. The future, once shrouded in uncertainty and shadows, now unfolded with the warmth of family and the anticipation of new beginnings.

And she couldn't wait to greet them.

The End

About the Author

Jennifer Seasons started her career writing contemporary romances for Avon and is the author of several popular contemporary and Regency historical romances. Born in California, Jennifer has lived all over the West and now resides in the mountains of Massachusetts with her husband and their children. A dog and several cats keep them company. A lover of autumn, cozy cardigans, and coffee, Jennifer can often be found writing her novels by hand in notebooks, bundled in said cardigan with a steaming mug of dark roast nearby. When she's not writing, Jennifer enjoys running, hiking with her family, gardening, and lounging in a comfy spot with a good book and a homemade chocolate chip cookie or two.

Amazon – https://www.amazon.com/stores/Jennifer-Seasons/author/B00D8GZ5EE
Twitter – https://twitter.com/JenniferSeasons